Ans	_____	M.L.	_____
ASH	_____	MLW	_____
Bev	_____		
C.C.	_____		
Dick	_____		
DRZ	_____		
ECH	_____		
ECS	_____		
Gar	_____	Pion.P.	_____
GRM	_____	Q.A.	_____
GSP	_____	Riv	_____
G.V.	_____	Ross	_____
Har	_____	S.C.	_____
JPCP	_____	St.A.	_____
KEN	_____	St.J	_____
K.L.	_____	St.Joa	_____
K.M.	_____	St.M.	_____
L.H.	_____	Sgt	_____
LO	_____	T.H.	_____
Lyn	_____	TLLO	_____
L.V.	_____	T.M.	_____
McC	_____	T.T.	_____
McG	_____	Ven	_____
McQ	_____	VP	_____
MIL	_____	Wat	_____
	_____	Wed	_____
	_____	WIL	_____

THE LUCK MACHINE

The world is surrounded by intangible energies of which man has little knowledge. Electricity, once an unsuspected natural force, is now a known reality . . . so why not luck? Once recognised as an actual force, the next step is to construct a machine to harness its forces. However, if one person attracts good luck, another is due for bad luck. And when the Luck Machine falls into the wrong hands, the inventors wish they'd stuck to rabbits' feet and black cats . . .

E. C. TUBB

THE LUCK MACHINE

Complete and Unabridged

LINFORD
Leicester

First published in Great Britain

First Linford Edition
published 2009

British Library CIP Data

Tubb, E. C.
   The luck machine- -(Linford mystery library)
   1. Science fiction.
   2. Large type books.
   I. Title II. Series
   823.9'14–dc22

ISBN 978–1–84782–791–3

Published by
F. A. Thorpe (Publishing)
Anstey, Leicestershire

Set by Words & Graphics Ltd.
Anstey, Leicestershire
Printed and bound in Great Britain by
T. J. International Ltd., Padstow, Cornwall

This book is printed on acid-free paper

To
JIM and DOROTHY RATIGAN

1

From the curve of the B2169, a mile from the village of Stark and a few furlongs past the pond at Willards Copse, the time-darkened brick and stucco of St Elmers private school for boys rose in sombre splendour behind the tall screen of elms marching behind the crumbling brick of the surrounding wall. A gate pierced the wall, flanked with scabrous pillars surmounted with roughly circular orbs of stone which could have been residual ammunition for some antediluvian cannon and beneath them, chipped and worn into indistinguishable configurations, carved heraldic designs made a pathetic boast of time-forgotten importance.

A battered, twenty-seater coach stood in the narrow road before the gate, the roof piled high with baggage, the interior stuffed with boys and, against one of the pillars, his face twisted into a strained, unnatural smile, stood a man. His name was Nigel Lloyd, he was a master at St Elmers and his thoughts belied his expression.

'Goodbye, sir!' shrilled a strident voice from the coach.

'Goodbye, Cary.'

'Have a nice holiday, sir!'

'Thank you, Cary.'

'Don't overdo it, sir!'

'I won't, Cary,' called Nigel. Then, under his breath, his expression still twisted into a smile, '*You sadistical little bastard!*'

'Goodbye, sir!'

'Goodbye, Moulton.'

'Goodbye, sir!'

'Goodbye, Evans.'

'Goodbye, sir!'

'Goodbye, Holt. *The little swine are getting me at it! Why the hell doesn't Innes get this wreck moving?*'

The driver must have been telepathic. To Nigel's relief the irregular pulse of the engine rose to a grinding snarl and, with a gush of evil-smelling exhaust, the coach drove away from the gate, the roar of the engine drowning out the final chorus of goodbyes. Dutifully Nigel waved farewell and then, as the vehicle rounded the bend, let the smile slip from his face and his features resume their normal expression.

It wasn't a contented one. There was cynicism in it and irony and some self-contempt but there was humour in it too, the wry amusement of a man who has admitted his own limitations and recognized himself as a failure. It went well with the shock of dark, overlong and always untidy hair, the shrewd grey eyes and the paint and chemical-stained corduroy jacket and trousers he wore and which were explained away to the parents of prospective pupils — when such explanations were a forced necessity — as the hallmark of an artistic and scientific genius too engrossed in his studies to spare concern for his outward appearance.

Lighting a cigarette he leaned against one of the pillars of the gate, half-wishing that he had ridden into the village where he could have dropped off for a drink, but he doubted that any amount of ale would have compensated for the prolonged presence of the boys and, even if it had, there would still have been the walk back. Later, perhaps, in the cool of the evening, he might make the effort. He might even have cause to celebrate.

It was a faint hope, too faint to be worth any real consideration, but it was nice to dream and he closed his eyes, enjoying the warmth of the summer sun and listening to the restless twitter of birds, the cigarette falling unnoticed from his fingers as his imagination soared on pinions, less tangible, but far less limited than those of the winged creatures above. He came to ground again, opening his eyes as heavy feet crunched the gravel at his side, knowing by the odour which stung his nostrils who it must be.

'Hullo, Norm.'

'I thought you were asleep.'

'I was thinking. I've come to the conclusion that I hate all boys.'

'You don't really mean that.' Norman Dale, thick and stocky in his shapeless tweeds, the jacket with the worn leather patches which were as much a uniform for the masters as the school cap and blazer were for the boys, took the oversized pipe from his mouth and gestured with it down the road. 'All gone?'

'Yes, thank God!'

'They gave you a rough time, eh?'

It was a magnificent understatement. Hell, thought Nigel grimly, must surely be patterned on the last few hours of term and Hell, when you were the master in charge of travel arrangements, came uncomfortably close.

Everyone had been against him. Pupils who had lost tickets, travel money, personal baggage and, apparently the ability to memorize the simplest instructions. Parents who had decided to collect their offspring and who had blithely arrived far too early and had waited in fuming impatience and others who had turned up carelessly late. Doting aunts and reminiscent uncles. Posturing elder sisters and condescending elder brothers whose arrogance was matched only by their ignorance. And boys! Boys who had seemed to have undergone a peculiar metamorphosis at the approach of freedom turning into young animals who would have tried the patience of a saint.

But it was all over now. The last consignment had been shipped out to home or perdition and a blissful peace had descended on the school.

'You let them get on top of you,' said Norman, drawing at his pipe. 'The trick is to remain utterly detached and to regard them as something not quite human. Experimental animals, perhaps, or a culture on an agar plate. Once you allow yourself to get flustered they sense it and from then on life can get a little difficult.'

Norman, thought Nigel, was full of understatements. Idly he wondered if any master had been driven to suicide by a mob of uncontrollable boys and then decided none. They would probably have reached a point of uncoordinated frenzy before discovering the simple way out and have been quietly led away. His face darkened at recent memory.

'Cary,' he said.

'Cary?' Norman frowned at his pipe. 'Oh, young Julian. What about him?'

'He's a little swine. He knows damn well that we're not going anywhere this holiday but he had to rub it in. I'll watch for our Julian next term.'

'I seem to remember that you watched for him last term,' said Norman drily. 'He was only getting his own back.'

'For having reported him to the Head for bullying?'

'For what you called bullying,' corrected Norman. 'As far as he was concerned he was only exercising the right of the strong to inflict his will on the weak. Did young Lomas complain?'

'He was too scared to.'

'Perhaps, or then again he was probably abiding by the code of schoolboy behaviour. I've told you before, Nigel, you can't afford to get too involved with the boys. Your mistake is that you regard them as human beings.'

'Well, aren't they?'

'Not in the sociological-cultural sense we use the word. No child is. They are primitives guided solely by the instinct of self-preservation. They only become what we choose to call human when they have

7

been conditioned to acceptance of our own framework of social behaviour. Most of the child psychologists would be out of work tomorrow if we recognized that children and adults are two entirely different species.'

Nigel looked dubious.

'Isn't that going a bit too far?'

'I don't think so, certainly not psychologically speaking. We expect a child to act, think and feel like an adult. How would you like to be forced to act, think and feel like a child?'

He drew at his pipe again, blew down the stem and sucked until his rotund cheeks developed twin hollows. Taking it from his mouth he stared into the bowl, scowled and jabbed at the contents with a blunt finger. Nigel watched with mounting interest.

'Still not right?'

'No. The coltsfoot and rosemary blend well enough but burn far too hot. I've tried adding heather, rose petals and some dried and powdered laurel to the basic mixture but the proportions can't be right. The damn stuff won't stay alight.'

Deliberately he knocked the dottle from the bowl and stuffed the pipe into a pocket. From another he produced a small plastic bag, checked the number scrawled on it then upended it, allowing the contents to scatter on the ground. Replacing the bag he produced a notebook, opened it and, with a pencil, made a final notation.

'Mixture thirty-two,' read Nigel over his shoulder. 'N.B.G. Now what?'

'Mixture thirty-three. Do you think I should add more laurel?'

'If you want to get into a state of what the ancients called ecstasy I'd smoke nothing else. That's what the old hags who ran the oracles used to do They chewed dried laurel, inhaled fumes from the same and then started to prophesy. Of course, if you really want to go up the wall you could add some leaves of Indian hemp, or dried poppy heads, the seeds of Morning Glory, mescal buttons or, if you'd prefer, I could recommend a few varieties of hallucinogenic fungi. They should really work.'

'I'm serious, Nigel.'

'So am I. You might be a whizz at psychology and a wonder at classical history and comparative religion but you're no scientist. The trouble with you amateurs is that, when you get started on a hobby, you simply don't recognize the dangers. Rhubarb leaves for example.'

'Well?'

'You had the brilliant idea of curing them and making a non-dutiable smoking mixture. The only thing was that you didn't know they were loaded with oxalic acid. If I hadn't been around you'd have poisoned yourself.' Nigel shook his head. 'Why don't you just give it up and smoke tobacco like the rest of us humans?'

'And rot my lungs with carcinogens? No thank you.'

Nigel didn't press the point as they walked from the gate towards the school. He liked the older man and, if he found enjoyment in his hobby, he didn't want to spoil it by pointing out that carcinogens weren't confined to the hot smoke from burning tobacco. But he hoped that Norman would soon hit on a mixture that was inoffensive to the nostrils.

Neither man hurried. Before them the crushed gravel of the quad stretched from the wall to the main building; once an old English manor house but now converted into a repository for boys. St Elmers wasn't unique, there were dozens of such private schools, small places for the most part, the majority of them taking full advantage of the fact that anyone, with or without qualifications, could open a school. St Elmers wasn't the worst of its kind but it was far from being the best and it was symbolic of Nigel's own station in life. Far, very far from the top but unpleasantly close to the bottom. It was an uncomfortable thought.

'There's Winnard,' said Norman abruptly. 'Now there's someone who has real cause to be grateful for the end of term.'

A man had come round the edge of the building from the direction of the kitchen. He was a squat, ape-like man with heavily tattooed arms, the faded designs revealed beneath the rolled-up sleeves of his collarless shirt. Thick, dark hair coated his arms and showed on his chest. Despite the heat he wore a stained waistcoat and a brass-studded belt circled his bulging waist. He rolled a little as he walked and, as he approached the two masters, he lifted his right hand to his forehead in a gesture common among naval men in the time of the wooden ships.

' 'Day, genelmen,' he muttered.

He wasn't drunk, not quite, but he was a long way from being sober. Norman shook his head as he stared after him.

'He's taking a chance. If the Head catches him like that he'll be in trouble.'

'He's been celebrating,' said Nigel, and he could guess why. Winnard was the butt of the school and, without the thin protective authority of a master, he was fair game to every boy with a twisted sense of humour. Life, for the school porter, must be an unremitting hell and it was little wonder that he flew to the bottle for relief. Nigel wondered where he kept it, with Mrs Beecham, his widowed sister and the resident cook, he supposed, but he couldn't ask and he would never be told. The thin line of class effectively prevented any social mixing between masters and servants.

'He's still taking a chance,' said Norman. It seemed to worry him. 'If he gets kicked out of here he'll never find another job.'

'He doesn't have to worry. There's always relief.'

Privately Nigel considered that the man would be better off on National Assistance than as gardener, porter, caretaker and general kick-around at the school but he didn't share Norman's fears that the Head would mete out instant dismissal if he discovered Winnard in his present state. The Head was no fool and would probably look the other way. He would have a hard time finding people to work as hard for so little as the porter and his sister and he knew it.

Thinking of money reminded Nigel of what he had to do.

'Leave it,' advised Norman when Nigel excused himself. 'I don't know what you want to see the Head about but leave it until after lunch.'

'I don't want to miss him.'

'You won't. He isn't leaving until late

13

afternoon and, anyway, Storm is in with him now.'

'Storm! Why?'

'He's breaking the good news.' A slow grin wreathed Norman's features. 'He's telling the old man that he won't be back next term.'

'He got the job then! The lucky devil!'

Storm was the junior English master and the Head had caught him fresh from University. He was a shy, introverted man with a slight stammer and had been too eager to commence repaying his parents for their financial sacrifices in subsidizing his higher education to look a gift horse in the mouth. Norman, Nigel knew, had been advising him to leave St Elmers at all costs and, apparently, the young man had taken his advice. Nigel hoped he would see it through.

'He will,' said Norman confidently when Nigel voiced his doubts. 'The job is signed, sealed and delivered. Not much more money than he is getting now but a damn sight better conditions and it won't hurt his reputation. It was a mistake for him ever to come here in the first place.

St Elmers is no credit to a young man starting his career.'

Or any other man no matter at what stage in his professional life, thought Nigel sourly.

'Where is he going?'

'Dumbarton technical college.' Norman fussed with his pipe. 'I know a man there.'

He didn't volunteer and Nigel didn't probe for further information. In many ways Dale was a bit of a mystery; his academic qualifications entitled him to a position far better than the one he held at St Elmers and it was generally assumed among the staff that he must have suffered some dreadful tragedy or ghastly scandal which had toppled him from the ranks of the respectably employed.

'Of course,' mused Nigel. 'Storm has a B.Sc and Ph.D as well as a B.A. Hell, he's as well qualified as I am.' He began to chuckle. 'The old man will have to get cracking if he hopes to replace him by next term. I bet he's hopping mad at the news.'

'You know the Head. He believes in loyalty; loyalty to the school, loyalty to himself, loyalty to the profession.'

'One sided loyalty,' reminded Nigel. 'There isn't one of us he wouldn't toss out at a day's notice if he could get someone to replace us at half the money. To hell with him, anyway. A man's got to look after himself in this world.'

He pursed his lips as he pondered the effect Storm's resignation would have on his own, personal problems. In one way it would be bad, the Head would be in a flaming temper and bitterly hurt at what he would regard as an underhanded trick but, on the other hand, he wouldn't be in too strong a position as regards riding roughshod over the rest of the staff. On the whole, Nigel decided, things were in his favour.

But there was one dubious factor.

'Maybe I'd better go in now,' he said. 'Hit him while the iron is hot.'

'You'd be a fool if you do,' advised Norman. 'There's no point in stacking the cards against yourself. Wait until after lunch. A hungry man is an irritable one, a well-fed one is usually contented.'

'That's what I'm worried about,'

16

admitted Nigel. 'It all depends on what Alice provides. If she's in one of her moods and serves up the swill she usually cooks . . . '

'Have you ever seen her serve the Head with the same food she cooks for the rest of us?'

'Well, no but . . . '

'Nor will she today. You can trust her to take care of him.' Norman glanced at his watch. 'Talking of lunch it's time we were eating. Let's go and see what our fair cook has provided.'

He strode towards the main door of the school then looked back as Nigel headed for the side of the building.

'Where are you going?'

'This way.'

There was always the chance, thought Nigel, as he led the way through the shrubbery, that he might discover where Winnard hid his supplies.

2

It had been a lousy lunch. Normally the masters, but never the Head whose digestion was a thing of tender delicacy, ate in the Hall with the boys, their presence not only a deterrent to horseplay and youthful wildness but to display the fact that their food, exactly the same as that served to the pupils, showed a gastronomic democracy which was appreciated by the parents if no one else. With the absence of the boys Nigel had hoped for the best. He had been grievously disappointed.

They had eaten in the common room, the communal resting place of the masters when off-duty, and even the trestle table with its white cloth had done little to offset the drabness of the brown-painted walls and yellowed ceiling, the fly-speckled prints and the dusty gowns which hung like flayed negroid skins on the pegs beside the door. The food would have earned Alice Beecham a moment's notice in any working-man's café, an assortment of semi-raw meat, undercooked potatoes and well-sanded cabbage swimming in a limpid pool of what she chose to call gravy. The sweet was a trifle of stale cake, stale jam, stale custard and was topped with synthetic cream — also stale.

The conversation matched the trifle.

Godfrey, the doyen of the school, had eaten in his usual whistling manner, shovelling the food down as if it was the last he hoped to eat before the resumption of school, interspersing his slobbers with shop talk wearying in its repetition. He, like Weight, was leaving for some unknown destination directly after the meal. Hill, younger but even more loquacious, was bubbling with his forthcoming continental holiday which would, Nigel thought moodily, turn out to be a caravan at Bognor or, more likely, a temporary job at some holiday camp. Blake was no better and May was an unmitigated pain in the neck. The only consolation was that, of them all, only he and Norman would be here for tea.

An hour later, after coffee which tasted of burnt acorns and a round of farewells which left him weak, Nigel went to test his luck.

An air of respectability hung around Phillip Martyn-Seabright D.D., B.A., B.Sc., and that same air of conventional trustworthiness reflected itself in the appointments of his study. Framed testimonials flanked signed photographs of the famous as they smirked down from the walls. The gilt titles of impressive-looking tomes threw back the light from the windows, their expensive leather bindings carefully scuffed to show much handling and silver cups, shields and medallions spoke mutely of past sporting prowess as did the scarred cricket bat and worn boxing gloves hanging over the fireplace.

It only needed a dog, thought Nigel disrespectfully, a hound of some kind, to complete the traditional picture of the perfect athlete-scholar, a huntin', shootin', fishin', type of reverend gentleman whose greatest joy was in riding to hounds and instilling knowledge and character into the boys placed in his charge.

But a dog would have shed hairs over the thick carpet and the image was good enough without the nuisance of a pet.

'Ah, Lloyd,' he said as Nigel entered the study. 'You want to see me?'

'Yes, sir.'

'It, ah, it isn't the most convenient of times, Lloyd.'

'It won't take a moment, sir.'

'Very well,' said the Head as if he were a sovereign graciously condescending to listen to a serf. 'But please be brief.'

The voice matched the man, the deep, rolling tones and perfect diction going well with the mane of snow-white hair and the smooth, round, unlined face. A pair of gold-rimmed pince-nez hung from a wide velvet ribbon around the neck and the Head had been known to terrify a pupil by simply resting them on his nose. He wore a tailored suit of clerical grey, a hand-made shirt and a tie which cost more than Nigel liked to think about.

'It's about my salary, sir,' he blurted.

'As you know the cost of living has risen quite a bit since we joined the school and Maida, that is the Matron, suggested that I have a word with you about it.'

'I should not like to think,' said the Head sonorously, 'that there was any matter which any of the staff could not speak to me about at any time.'

A tray rested on the desk beside him containing the remains of a lunch. The edge of a fillet steak joined the remains of thin fried potatoes, mushrooms and tomatoes. The sweet had been fresh strawberries and cream. A glass stood beside the empty coffee cup and, as the Head picked it up, Nigel's nostrils caught the odour of brandy. The swine, he knew, was playing for time.

'An excellent vintage,' murmured the Head as he set down the empty glass. Delicately he touched a napkin to his lips.

'You appreciate good brandy, Lloyd?'

'When I can afford it, sir, yes.'

'Ah, of course.' Leaning back the Head half-closed his eyes. 'You have been with us for how long now? A year?'

'Two years, sir.'

'A pleasant association, I trust?'

'Yes, but — '

'I understand.' The lifted hand was a studied gesture of elegance. 'Tell me, Lloyd, was it not Sophocles who said that a scholar should be content to wear rags and eat herbs if by so doing he could continue to teach?'

'I doubt it,' said Nigel drily. 'But if he did he fully merited what happened to him. The labourer is worthy of his hire, sir.'

'True. True, but the principle is a good one. We have a grave duty you and I, Lloyd. Into our care are placed the empty vessels which it is our charge to fill to the brim with knowledge and send armed and armoured into the world outside. It is no small responsibility we have undertaken. The profession of which we are proud members has long been above mere considerations of self and sordid financial gain. I tell you, Lloyd, that I should be well content to follow the dictates of that old Greek philosopher and to wear rags and eat the bread of charity if there was no other way to follow my calling. And, Lloyd, I expect those with me here at St Elmers to feel the same.'

The old hypocrite, thought Nigel bitterly, was certainly in good form.

'I'm sorry, sir, but — '

'Can it be, Lloyd, that you disagree with those high principles?'

'No, sir, of course not, but things aren't as simple as that. For one thing the bread of charity seems to be conspicuous by its absence and, after all, we have to think of our future. Maida . . . Matron and I aren't as young as we were and we'd like to know our position.'

'Age!' sighed the Head. 'Anno Domini — it comes on us all. But you aren't an old man yet, Lloyd.'

'I'm thirty-seven.'

'And Matron is seven years younger.' The Head nodded as if he had solved a knotty problem. 'Both young, both in the prime of life, both with so much still to give. How fortunate you are!'

Nigel hesitated, wondering just what to say and then decided to say nothing. Somehow the old man had neatly managed to evade the issue in a smoke-screen of verbosity and obviously thought he had managed to get away with it. Ostentatiously he glanced at the thin, gold watch strapped to his wrist.

'Well, Lloyd, I have enjoyed our little chat but *tempus fugit*, you know. I have much to occupy me before I leave and I am sure that you have matters requiring your personal attention.'

'Yes, sir,' said Nigel doggedly. 'Our salary. Can we hope for an increase and, if so, how much?'

It was curt, crude and to the point, three things the Head disliked because such a question demanded an answer and he hated to be pinned down. His irritation registered itself on the slight flush on his sallow cheeks and the way he toyed with his pince-nez.

'You have heard about Storm?' he asked abruptly.

'Only rumours, sir.'

'He is leaving us. Without notice, without consideration, without any of the common courtesies one usually associates with a member of our high profession. I cannot tell you, Lloyd, how shocked, even horrified I was to learn of his intentions.'

'Is that wholly fair, sir? Surely he had the right to terminate his engagement at end of term?'

'Legally you are no doubt correct but there are higher, moral issues than legalistic quibbles. There is such a thing as gratitude, Lloyd.'

'Yes, sir.'

'And loyalty to the school.'

'I agree, sir.'

'I am glad to hear it. I have been observing you of late and there have been many occasions when it seemed that you held St Elmers in a cynical regard which — but never mind that now. We all have our little individual quirks of character and I am a tolerant man as I think you have cause to know.'

'Yes, sir,' said Nigel woodenly. Trust the old fox to bring that up!

'Storm can be replaced, of course,' continued the Head blandly. 'There are many qualified men on the register of the agency, too many really for the health of the profession, but I always dislike introducing new masters if it can be avoided. It tends to disturb the boys and to unsettle that wonderful gestalt we have here at St Elmers.'

'I understand, sir.'

'It warms my heart that you do. I have always maintained that . . . '

His voice droned on but Nigel wasn't listening. He had heard it all before, in one form or another, to the parents of prospective pupils and the visiting parents of boys who had had their doubts as to the worth of the school. He was more concerned with what had immediately preceded the present monologue.

It had been smooth, he had to admit that. The false sentiment, the artificial indignation, the hidden reminder and the covert threat and all adding up to a great big refusal. No rise, no more money, no cause to celebrate at all. Idly he wondered what Maida would say when he told her then became aware that the droning monologue had ceased and that the Head was waiting for an answer to something he had said.

'Uh, I beg your pardon, sir?'

'I said that I hoped you and Matron would enjoy this break from your normal routine.'

'We hope to, sir.'

'Ah, teaching, teaching, it demands so much from us all!' The Head glanced at his watch again. 'Well, Lloyd, I really must terminate this little chat. Were there any other trifles you wished to clear up before I leave?'

'No, sir.' If trying to get enough money to live on was what the Head chose to call a trifle he wondered what something important would have to be. Probably the loss of a couple of pupils or an overdone steak. The Head smiled as he saw Nigel glance at the tray.

'I wonder if you would run this tray down to the kitchen. Mrs Beecham has had a pretty hectic day, one way and another and we must consider those called to serve beneath us.'

Nigel didn't move.

'The tray, Lloyd.'

Slowly Nigel picked it up, hesitating as he fought the impulse to smash it down on the white-maned head, knowing that

28

to do so would give him the utmost satisfaction but knowing too what the consequences would be. Almost he disregarded them then, mouth tense, he carried it towards the door. He simply wasn't in a position to afford ungoverned displays of emotion.

'Lloyd!'

He halted in the passage outside, turning to see the bland smile of the Head beyond the open portal.

'The door, Lloyd. Please close the door.'

Carefully Nigel set down the tray and closed the door. Carefully he picked up the tray again and walked from the study. He didn't kick anything until he reached the stairs.

Mrs Beecham was alone in the kitchen when he arrived. Savagely he slammed down the tray and faced the cook.

'Why the hell can't we have food like that?'

'Don' ask me, sir,' she said in her slurring voice. ' 'Tis Mr Martyn-Seabright what gives the orders.'

'What orders?'

'You know full well, sir. Masters are to eat the same as the boys.'

'That's during term. Why can't we have decent food during the vacation?'

'I do my best I'm sure, sir.'

'Some best!' sneered Nigel. 'Where the hell did you learn to cook, in jail?'

''Tis not nice of you to say that, sir, and you know it. I'm a respectable widow woman, I am, and you've no call to carry on so.'

She was a drab of a woman, thin and stooped with mousey hair and a great mole on her left cheek from which sprouted a cluster of hairs. Her eyes were usually devoid of expression but now, to Nigel's horror, they began to glisten with tears.

'There, there!' He clumsily patted her on one bony shoulder. 'I didn't mean it. Don't upset yourself.'

'I've never been in prison, sir. Never.'

'I'm sure you haven't.'

'I'm a decent woman, sir, always have been.'

'I know that.' Privately he thought that, with her face and figure, she couldn't have had much opportunity to be anything else. 'I was just in a temper. Please forget it.'

'Something wrong?' Norman stepped into the kitchen, mixture number thirty-three throwing a pungent cloud of smoke before him. Glad of the interruption Nigel left the snuffling woman and joined his friend. He hesitated then, yielding to the pressure of Norman's hand, allowed himself to be guided from the kitchen.

'There's nothing you can do when a woman gets into that state,' advised Norman. 'It's best just to leave her alone to get over it. What happened, anyway?'

'The Head got my back up. The old goat touched me on the raw and I suppose I was getting my own back on Alice, the poor bitch.'

'A common form of substitution,' soothed Norman. 'Most people take it out on the wrong person when they can't hurt the one who has hurt them. Well, perhaps it's all for the best. She can take it better than Maida. How is she by the way?'

'I don't know. She went to bed with a

31

sick headache long before lunch and I haven't seen her since.' Nigel drew a deep breath. 'Well, I suppose I'd better see how she is and break the unhappy news. I can just imagine how she'll take it.'

'No luck, eh?'

'Luck,' said Nigel bitterly, 'is something I've never had. Never in my whole life. Never!'

He was wrong, thought Norman as he strode away. It was lucky at least that Maida hadn't heard his last remark.

Maida was up when Nigel entered her room. Even though they were legally married they were officially supposed to sleep apart and certainly, because of the cramped beds supplied, there was little choice if either wanted to get some rest. In any case St Elmers didn't care for the delights of connubial bliss and the Head had refused Nigel's suggestion that he obtain a double bed with a shocked; 'Impossible! What would the boys think!'

What the boys thought Nigel didn't care. What did concern him was the distance apart of their respective rooms which made him feel, as he had once said to Norman, 'like a smooching porter in a third rate hotel.'

Norman had laughed and pointed out that the atmosphere of stealth and romance surrounding the arrangement could only be good for the marriage. But it hadn't worked out like that.

'Hello,' he said brightly as he entered the room. 'How's the head?'

'Splitting.'

'Shall I kiss it to make it better?'

'Leave me alone, Nigel!' She squirmed in his grasp as he tried to kiss the top of her head. 'Don't be such a fool!'

'All right.' He slumped on the edge of the bed and lit a cigarette as he stared at his wife. She was sitting before the dressing table dressed in her underwear which, though scrupulously clean, wasn't as new as it might have been. She wasn't hard to look at with her firm, slim, rounded figure and it was only the fine lines around her eyes and the hard set of her lips which betrayed her disposition.

'Well?'

'Well what?'

'You know what I mean.' She pursed

her lips and carefully applied make-up. 'Did you get it?'

'No.'

'No?' She put down the lipstick and dabbed her mouth with tissue. The mascara was next and then a touch of eye-shadow. Maida, Nigel thought, was celebrating the end of term in her own way. Normally she had to be careful of the amount of cosmetics she used for fear of inflaming the dormant sexual impulses of the pupils. At least that was the theory but Nigel thought she, and he, had more to fear from the repressed impulses of the masters in their semi-monastic existence.

'That's what I said.' He blew smoke towards her and watched it curl around her head. 'No rise. Period.'

'I might have guessed,' she said bitterly. Rising she picked up her dress and held it before her. It had never been an expensive garment and now was far worse than cheap. It was out of fashion.

'That looks nice,' said Nigel weakly. She glared her scorn.

'It's a rag and you know it but, because I happened to marry a man without a spine it seems I'll have to wear it the rest of my life. Why didn't you insist?'

'We have a home here.' His gesture included the school. 'We have beds, food and some form of comfort. It was made pretty clear to me that we would lose the little we have if I didn't yield. So I yielded.'

'Coward! No wonder the Head doesn't respect you.'

'The Head only respects himself.'

'Do you expect me to go on living like this for the rest of my life?'

'You can do what you damn well please!'

'Nigel! How dare you talk to me like that!'

'Keep your voice down,' he snapped. 'There's no need to let everyone know how much in love we are.'

'Love!'

'Yes, love. Married couples are supposed to be in that happy state you know. And why did you lock your door last night?'

'I was tired.'

'You've been tired for the past five weeks.'

'Men!' She wriggled into her dress. 'That's all you think about!'

'Can you blame us?'

He caught her around the hips, his hands preventing the fall of her dress, and drew her towards him. Snatching up a hairbrush she rapped him smartly on the top of the head.

'Hell!'

'Leave me alone! You know I hate to be mauled about.'

'Since when?'

She ignored his sneer, carefully arranging the dress about her figure. Nigel, massaging his scalp, felt his momentary tenderness turn into active dislike.

'You don't like anything,' he said bitterly. 'All you want out of life is a nice wardrobe, a well-trained provider and all the time in the world to mess about with your face and figure. God knows what for if you don't want anyone to admire it.'

'If I wanted all those things,' she said acidly, 'I was disappointed, wasn't I?' She gestured about the room. 'Look at what you've provided for me. A twenty-four hour a day job, food I wouldn't feed to a pig, clothes that are a laugh and a husband who is a contemptible failure. Heaven knows why I married you.'

'You married me because you thought you were pregnant,' he said brutally. 'Or you made me think you were. I was a good catch in those days, wasn't I?'

He had gone too far and knew it when he saw her brimming eyes. One thing about Maida, no matter how justifiably angry he became with her the sight of her tears could always make him feel ashamed of himself. And, he supposed, she did have a right to despise him, at times he despised himself. It wasn't much of a life he had provided for her, far less than she had been led to expect, but even so she didn't have to make things worse than what they were.

'I'm sorry,' he apologized. 'I shouldn't have said that.'

'Why not, if you think it's true.' She spoke in the hard, casual, offhand and unforgiving tone which jarred his nerves and made him grit his teeth.

'Please let's not quarrel, Maida. I've said I'm sorry, can't we leave it at that?'

'For how long?' She stared hard into his eyes. 'Listen to me, Nigel. Last year you promised that we would get out of here at end of term. That was a year ago. This year you said we'd have more money and that was a lie too. Well, my mind is made up. If you don't do something to get us out of here before next term I'm leaving you.'

'Where will you go?'

'That doesn't matter.'

'Maida! You can't be serious!'

'You'll see.'

He shrugged as she turned away, not really taking the threat seriously because she had threatened similar action before, but not liking the tone of the conversation. Maida would only leave him if she had a strong enough incentive and that presupposed someone who would be willing to provide for her better than he could. Mentally he reviewed the potential dangers at St Elmers and dismissed them one after the other. Certainly none of the masters had anything better to offer and the Head was too wary of scandal to become involved. The boys were out of the question. A parent, perhaps? One of the gruff-voiced uncles? He doubted it. The opportunities for social contact were too limited for anything of that nature to develop and he knew Maida well enough to know that she would never settle for a casual affair. With her it would be all or nothing.

He sighed and relaxed then tensed again as he spotted the corner of an envelope sticking from behind the mirror.

'What's this? A letter?'

'It's for you.' She handed it to him. 'Eric fetched it back with him from Stark.'

'Good old Robbie,' said Nigel thumbing open the flap. 'Always ready to do his fellow man a good turn.' He read the letter, turned it over and read it again. 'It's from Ted. Ted Bain, you remember him?'

'I — '

'You must remember him!' He was excited, his voice rising with enthusiasm. 'That time when he took us out and hit that taxi with his car. You remember how he pretended to be a foreigner when the police arrived.'

'I remember,' she said distastefully.

'And that time when . . . '

'Yes, yes, I remember him. What about it?'

'He's coming to St Elmers! He wants to see us. He should be here tomorrow!'

3

He arrived in a wreck of a car during a
rainstorm which did its best to maintain
the reputation of the English summer, the
locked wheels sending a shower of gravel
from the soaking drive as he drew to a
halt outside the main doors of the school.
Nigel, who had been waiting with
mounting impatience, ran down to meet
him as his long, ungainly form emerged
from the vehicle.

'Ted!'

'Nigel! Man, it's good to see you!'

They stood, gripping hands, grinning
like fools in the rain before Nigel
remembered to lead him inside. He liked
Ted. There was a casual vivacity about
him which turned everything solemn into
something comic and the most tragic
occasions were, to him, matters of
amusing comment. He was an unprepos-
sessing figure, well over six feet tall and
not above a hundred and sixty pounds in

weight, he wore thick-lensed spectacles and had long and shaggy hair. But his clothes, though rumpled, were good and the keenness of his brain belied his appearance.

'Maida!' He advanced towards her, hand outstretched. 'You look lovelier every time I see you.'

'Hello, Ted.'

She held out her hand to be shaken and blinked when, instead of the normal gesture, he lifted it to his lips and kissed the back of her hand.

'I saw that in a film,' he said. 'It is supposed to be loaded with erotic significance but, whenever I've tried it, I get a scream of mirth or a patrician glare.' He looked at Maida. 'Ah, the patrician glare. Well, you always were a lady.'

'You're a fool,' she said with amusement. 'Did you have a nice trip?'

'Two punctures and a seized water-pump. Is there anywhere I can dump my things, Nigel? The roof leaks.'

'Bring them inside.' Nigel peered at the car through the rain. 'Have you very much?'

'All I own.'

'All — ?' He glanced at Ted's face and saw that he wasn't joking. 'I'd better help you then. We can put them into Storm's old room.'

Despite what Ted had said there wasn't all that much luggage. Three quick trips and they had it all neatly stacked in the cramped quarters of the departed master, the baggage making it look more like a human habitation than a condemned cell. Ted sat on the bed, tested the springs and gave a soundless whistle.

'Are they all like this?'

'Worse.'

'Then I must be lucky.' Ted produced cigarettes and passed them to Nigel. 'Is it all right if I stay here for a while?'

'Stay?'

'That's what I said.'

'But what about your job?'

'I got kicked out.' Ted frowned at the smoke of his cigarette. 'Take warning, Nigel, never joke with an establishment dealing with secret developments. They have absolutely no sense of humour.'

'So?'

'So I forgot that. We had a fat slob in the department, Guthrie, you may have heard of him. No? Well you don't want to. He fancies himself as a scientist but what he knows about sub-atomic particles you could put in your eye and never know it was there. Anyway, everyone knew that the fool was a barrier to progress; he simply refused to admit that anything new has been discovered since Eddington and we were getting some peculiar results from a series of tests I had suggested might bear fruit. So I decided that it would be a good idea if our friend were to be quietly removed to a place where he couldn't gum up the works any longer.'

'How did you manage that?'

'Simplicity itself. I arranged to have a lot of Communist literature delivered to him, *The Daily Worker*, that sort of thing, and some postcards with Russian stamps on them. I got the stamps from a sixpenny packet. Well, knowing how the mind of security works I knew that it was only a matter of time before they would get suspicious and move him to some innocuous position.'

'And did they?'

'Oh, they got suspicious all right, but the whole thing backfired. They found out that I was the brain behind the propaganda and had me on the carpet for it.' He solemnly shook his head. 'That's what I meant when I said about not having a sense of humour. They simply refused to believe that it was all a harmless joke. They insisted that I tell them who had paid me to seduce Guthrie from his loyalties and suspended me while they check my background.'

'Suspended? But you said that you'd been kicked out.'

'I will be when they find out I joined the Commies fifteen years ago.' He chuckled at Nigel's expression. 'Don't look so startled. I'm no rebel or spy. It was just that I stopped to listen to one of their speakers and there was this girl, all hair and legs and you-know-what and, well, I signed up just to get close to her. It's all lies anyway. They don't believe in sharing everything. She didn't anyway.'

'Maybe you weren't dedicated enough?' suggested Nigel.

'Maybe not, but it'll damn me when they find out.' He stretched back on the bed and blew smoke towards the ceiling. 'That's why I was hoping I could stay here for a few weeks. Lay low, as it were. Possible?'

'Perhaps.' Nigel was dubious. 'Are you telling me the truth?'

'Nigel! Would I ever lie to an old friend?'

'Yes. Your story stinks. It sounds to me as if you've got some poor bitch into trouble and want to take it on the run until it blows over. Right?'

'Wrong. The truth is that I'm on the run from my creditors. Better?'

Nigel shrugged and gave up. Ted had a simple defence against curiosity, he told so many plausible but conflicting stories that it was impossible to know which was the truth if any, but whatever the reason Nigel would be glad to have him around if it could be arranged. Ted saw no objection.

'Who's to know?'

'The cook for one, her brother for another. Maida's all right and so is

Norman but Robbie may blow the gaff.'

'On what?' Ted's eyes were guileless behind his spectacles. 'You tell the cook that the Head has given his permission for me to be here. You tell Robbie the same. Only you don't stick your neck out all the way. You don't say that the Head told you direct, you say that you understand that things are as you say. The cook has no reason to question the Head about it and, if this Robbie does, you tell the old man you thought I was a guest of Robbie's, whoever he is.' He spread his hands. 'Simple.'

'Well . . . '

'Look on it as a challenge,' urged Ted as the serpent must have urged in the Garden. He glanced at his wristwatch. 'What time do you eat around here, anyway? I'm starving.'

'There will be something called dinner in half-an-hour,' said Nigel looking at his own watch. 'I hope you enjoy it.'

Maida was with Norman when they arrived and Nigel introduced the two men. Ted wrinkled his nose at the odour from the pipe then recovered and Nigel left them talking of crippling taxation, the merits of leaves as a substitute for tobacco and the habits of some South American tribe who smoked cigars as thick as a broom handle made from some local vegetation. Maida plucked his arm.

'What's he going to eat? Alice has only catered for the four of us.'

'Where's Robbie?'

'I don't know. He went back into the village.'

'Good, that means he won't be back for dinner. Ted can eat his.'

He was being optimistic. If lunch the previous day had been bad this dinner was infinitely worse. Nigel thought regretfully of the salad they had had at midday — there was a limit, at least, to the abuse raw vegetables could take, but this — !

'What is it?' Ted looked down at his plate.

'I should think that it represents steak and kidney pie.' Norman dug in his fork and examined a lump of gristle skewered on the end. 'Some form of animal, anyway.'

'Is it dead?'

'I should rather be inclined to say that it is.'

'Well, dead or not, I can't eat it.' Ted pushed aside his plate. Norman shook his head.

'Not that way,' he advised. 'First you break up the potatoes so that they will not be served up fried for breakfast. Of course, you can't be sure they won't arrive as mash later in the week or disguised in a shepherds pie, but at least you can take elementary precautions.' He set an example by wielding his fork on his own tubers. 'Raw,' he snorted. 'Hard as bullets right through. Really, something will have to be done about Alice.'

'The cook?' Ted jerked his head towards the kitchen.

'Yes.'

'Young, plump and inexperienced?'

'Old, withered and inexperienced.'

'I see.' Ted looked thoughtful. 'Maybe I can do something about the situation. Should I be a visiting inspector from the Ministry of Health? An inspector from the Ministry of Education? Or just a

convivial, simple soul? The latter, I think.'
He rose and left the room, returning with
the neck of a flat bottle protruding from
his pocket. He winked at them as he
vanished towards the kitchen.

'Bribery,' mused Norman. 'It never
fails.'

'It can't turn a silk purse into a sow's
ear or make a good cook from a bad.'

'We'll see,' said Maida with a woman's
instinct. She smiled at Ted as he rejoined
them, his pocket empty. 'Well?'

'Well.' He sat down and beamed at the
others. 'It's too late to do anything now
but she promises me that things will be
different tomorrow after she has been to
the shops. In the meantime there is
always bread and cheese.' He helped
himself liberally and nodded towards the
kitchen. 'You know, that poor woman in
there is a very misunderstood creature.
She has had some terrible luck in life.'

'Haven't we all?' Nigel was sour.

'Perhaps, but hers has been all of the
negative kind. In other words all her luck
has been bad.'

'And mine hasn't, I suppose?'

'No. Yours has been mostly neutral and some positive thrown in.' He smiled at Maida. 'In fact I'd be tempted to say that you've had more than your fair share of good fortune. How many men can boast of having such an attractive wife?'

Nigel grunted over his bread and cheese and Norman puffed a thoughtful cloud of aromatic smoke towards the visitor.

'You talk as if luck was a tangible thing.'

'Well, in a way it is, isn't it? As tangible as say, gravity or magnetism.'

'How do you make that out?'

'The only thing we know about gravity is that it exists, agreed?'

'Agreed.'

'Right, and we know that luck exists too, don't we?'

'Well . . .'

'We talk of good luck and of bad luck,' Ted continued. 'We even wear, some of us, good luck charms and we tend to select certain 'lucky' numbers if we enter a raffle. We talk of old so-and-so being a 'lucky' devil and of someone else as having no 'luck' at all. No, Norman, you can't tell me that we don't acknowledge the existence of something we call luck.'

'All right, I'll go along with you that far, but isn't it all superstition?'

'Magnetism was superstition once. A devil lived in lodestone and tried to eat iron, at least it drew it towards itself and for what other reason? Or gravity, it would be interesting to know what explanation the ancients gave to the habit of things to fall to the lowest point. Maybe they thought that demons sucked them down.'

'The two things aren't the same at all,' protested Norman. 'Gravity is an observable phenomena, so is magnetism. We may not know just what they are but we do know they exist.'

'So, don't you agree luck is an observable phenomena?'

'No.'

'How do you account for the fact that some men are born lucky and some the reverse?'

'Coincidence.'

'The same coincidence which will

permit one man to fall from the top of a building and escape with minor bruises and yet another will trip over a kerb and break his neck?' Ted shook his head. 'No, Norman, you can't disprove what I say by blaming it all onto coincidence. Luck, whether you admit it or not, is a real though as yet inexplicable force.'

'I'll believe that when I see it,' said Norman doggedly. 'Talking about a thing doesn't make that thing real and neither does putting a label on a phenomena make that phenomena what the label says it is. So we talk of luck, I'll admit that, but for all you know the thing we call luck needn't be the same thing at all.' He jabbed the stem of his pipe at the tall man.

'Two men fight,' he snapped. 'One kills the other. Luck?'

'For the one who survived, yes.'

'And the other?'

'Still luck, but bad this time, negative instead of positive.'

'Negative and positive! Like electricity?'

'Perhaps, as yet we don't really know.' Ted hesitated. 'Look, let us agree on what luck really is. Let's assume that it is a favourable selection of probabilities. I'm talking of good luck.'

'I'm not with you.'

'Let's take an example. A would-be suicide lifts a pistol to his head and pulls the trigger. Two things, assuming the gun to be loaded, can then happen. The cartridge fires or it misfires. If it fires — bang — the man's luck is bad and he's dead. If it misfires then the man's luck is good, in fact more than good, he has a charmed life.'

'Black and white,' murmured Norman. 'Black and white.' He jabbed with his pipe again. 'The gun could fire and then what? Simple finish?'

'Certainly not. Once again there is a choice. His aim could be excellent — and he dies. It could be bad and he only wounds himself.'

'Favourable probabilities,' said Nigel. 'I've read about that somewhere.'

'I don't understand what you're all talking about,' said Maida. She stifled a yawn. 'Are we going to sit here and talk of weird things all evening?'

'No.' Nigel, perhaps because of Ted's undisguised admiration, was immediately concerned. 'We'll walk down to the village.'

'Walk? And me with a car?'

'Is that what you call that wreck?' Nigel glanced at Maida. 'Would you trust yourself in it?'

'I think it's very nice of Ted to offer to drive us,' said Maida sharply. 'If you think I like walking a couple of miles in high heels you're sadly mistaken.'

'Put on your highest heels and fairest fabrics,' said Ted, 'and I'll go and start the banger. Coming, men?'

It had stopped raining but the air was damp and with an unseasonable chill and the prospect of a long walk was far from inviting. They settled themselves in the car, Nigel and Norman in the rear, Maida beside the driver, and relaxed in blissful comfort.

'Favourable probabilities,' murmured Norman as Ted reached for the starting button. 'It either starts or it doesn't.'

It didn't.

'Damn!' Ted thrust at the little plastic

knob. 'It must be jammed.'

'Anything I can do?' Nigel rested his hand on the handle of the door.

'No. I'll soon fix it.'

'More probabilities,' mused Norman. 'He either frees the starter or he doesn't.' He smiled at the sound of muttered cursing. 'Apparently his luck is negative. Or maybe he's just a lousy mechanic. You can't free a jammed starter the way he's trying to do.' He slid from the car. 'Have you got a starting handle?'

'The son-of-a-bitch-who-designed-this-model-didn't-believe-in-starting-handles!' Ted slammed down the hood. 'Damn the luck! We're stuck!'

'Negative luck?' Norman laughed with quiet amusement. 'Well, let Nigel and I add our positive luck to the situation. Right Nigel?'

Together they rocked the car until the starter freed itself. Norman nodded to the driver.

'Try it now.'

The engine roared to life.

'A skilful application of the principles of favourable circumstances,' mused Norman as they re-entered the car. 'Our luck is obviously good while yours, my friend, is bad. Of course, you could say that luck had nothing to do with it, that it was merely the application of a little muscle and a smattering of mechanical knowledge, but that would spoil the theory, wouldn't it?'

'You,' said Ted, 'are obviously the kind of man who demands proof.'

'Well, it does help.'

'In that case I shall give it to you.' He sent the car roaring down the narrow road towards Stark.

4

There were two pubs in the village, one a small, smoke-grimed hovel which dated from the time when Stark was a hamlet hugging the foot of the hill on which stood the Norman church and the other, by far the more modern and more popular, which carried the proud name of the local aristocrat. The Duke of Colborn wasn't so much popular because it was new as because of the landlord's daughter, a young woman by the name of Susan who was fully conscious of her attractions and was addicted to the wearing of loose, low-cut blouses and a habit of leaning over the bar.

'Nice,' said Ted appreciatively. 'Very nice.'

He could have been talking about the bar which was a happy blend of ancient and modern with its oaken panelling serving as a background for an assortment of copper cooking utensils, horse brasses, antique weapons and a scattering of curiosa which would have baffled any student of the past, but Nigel didn't think so. His next words qualified his suspicion.

'Forward my happy crusaders! Let us storm the breastworks!'

'Oh, sir!' Susan dimpled and lifted herself a full inch from the bar. A simple creature, despite her earthy wisdom, she laboured beneath the illusion that all professionals were men of inexhaustible wealth. Ted did nothing to disabuse her.

'Three double scotches,' he breathed, leaning close in case she was deaf. 'Three ales for chasers and a large, dry sherry. Is my memory good, Maida?'

She nodded.

'That's what comes of having an elephant for a father. And, of course, something for yourself.'

'Oh, sir!' The dimples became even more pronounced. 'You are a one! I'll have a small gin and lime if you don't mind.'

'Be a devil and have a large one,' suggested Ted. He raised his glass. 'Right, a toast. To Maida — and the one who

59

finishes last buys the next round!'

'Your friend,' said Norman about an hour later, 'seems to be quite a character.'

'They must think so.' Nigel gestured towards the regulars who, after their first, incredulous examination of the antics of the tall man, had decided to extend to him the customary courtesy with which they treated all foreigners. They ignored him.

'Odd,' mused Norman. 'He can't really be such a fool as he acts.'

'He isn't.' Nigel stared towards his friend where he leaned against the bar in deep conversation with Maida. 'That's just a façade. He's got a sharp mind and knows how to use it. No buffoon would have got the job he has — had.'

'Had?'

'He told me that he walked out but you can never be sure if Ted is telling the truth or spinning a line. He's with the atomic energy commission in some capacity or another. Whatever he does it's damn well paid.'

'The evidence seems to bear out that remark,' said Norman. 'If he keeps this up

Susan will want him to adopt her.'

'He would make a good catch for a mercenary female,' agreed Nigel absently, then became very thoughtful.

Narrowly he studied the couple at the bar. Ted, his ungainly length sprawled against the polished wood, had his head turned away so that Nigel couldn't see his face but he appeared to be talking with unusual seriousness. Maida, her profile in silhouette against the bottles ranked at the back of the bar, was listening with an attentiveness which Nigel found strange and a little disturbing. She hadn't paid him as much attention for years and it was hard to imagine what the tall man could be saying to warrant such absorption. Hard but not impossible.

'Where are you going?' Norman looked up as Nigel rose to his feet.

'Over to collect the others. How did they get over there anyway?'

'Maida went to powder her nose. Ted met her by the bar when he went over to get more drinks.'

'I'll help him carry them.' Nigel walked towards the couple noticing, not for the first time that evening, how attractive Maida could appear when she put her mind to it. She had always been a beautiful woman and ten years of marriage hadn't spoiled that beauty in any way. But now she seemed to actually scintillate as if she were trying very hard to impress someone and, Nigel knew, that someone couldn't be himself.

'We're dying of thirst,' he complained as he reached the others. 'Where are those drinks, Ted?'

'Just coming up.' He gestured towards the attentive barmaid. 'Maida and I were just catching up on local gossip.'

'Nice for you,' said Nigel drily. 'Did she tell you how wildly happy we are at St Elmers?'

'No one could be happy at that dump.' Ted passed Nigel his drink. 'Brown paint, hard beds, polished wood floors — talk about Dotheboys Hall!'

'The Head likes it well enough.'

'I'll bet he does.' Ted gathered up the rest of the drinks and headed back towards where Norman sat patiently waiting. 'I've seen the set-up before. The boys do all the work.' He mimicked a deep, rolling, pompous tone. 'We believe in the building of character here at St Elmers. The boys live a simple life of almost Spartan severity. They make their own beds, keep their own quarters in order and learn the basic qualities of self-sufficiency.' He returned to his normal tones. 'Right?'

'Right,' agreed Maida. 'The parents lap it up. Everyone likes to believe in the merits of Spartan simplicity as long as it isn't applied to themselves. In fact, of course, the poor little blighters do all the work including helping in the garden and the kitchen. Talk about a racket! The parents actually pay the Head for using their sons as servants.'

'Well,' said Ted philosophically. 'Times change but human nature never will. Squeers is still with us.' He lifted his glass. 'Here's to Squeers — God rot him!'

They drank.

'I'll get some more!' Ted, Nigel thought, drank like a fish and he found it hard to keep up. Determinedly he finished his own glass.

'No, I'll get them.'

'But — '

'I insist. Scotch, Norman? Ted? Sherry, Maida?' He answered their nods with one of his own, collected the empty glasses and walked to the bar. The unaccustomed alcohol had worked fast on his empty stomach and he felt a little lightheaded. Food and a wash, he thought, would soon restore him to normal and he decided on both. Food, in the shape of meat pies, could be bought over the bar but a wash necessitated a visit to the small back room. Setting down the glasses and grinning at Susan he headed towards the toilet.

He washed, gurgling and gargling as he rinsed his mouth, letting the water run as cold as it was going to before laving his face and neck. Carefully he combed his hair and wondered if he should get it cut before next term. Then, spruced and feeling a little more alert, he reached for the door.

It opened as he reached it and banged into his face.

'Damn and blast!' Nigel staggered back holding his nose. 'Why the hell can't you be more careful!'

'Sorry,' muttered the offender, a middle-aged man in a hurry. The door of the small compartment slammed decisively behind him.

Fuming Nigel bathed his nose, gratified to find that, at least, it wasn't broken. It wasn't even bleeding though, from the way it felt, it should have been. Irritably he thrust his way through the door and back into the bar, and groaned.

Eric Wilding had entered the room.

There was no way to avoid him, none at all and Nigel inwardly flinched as his colleague marched in his mechanical way towards him. No one, at the school, with the exception of Maida and the Head, ever called Eric by his right name. To everyone else he was Robbie and, looking at him, Nigel thought that never had a nickname been more apt.

There was something oddly robotic about him, even his eyes behind their thick lenses had a fixed and penetrating glare, and, when he moved, his arms and legs seemed almost to jerk with mechanical stiffness as if operated by gears and cams instead of blood and muscle. He was tall and thickly built with a prominent paunch and a peculiarly shaped head undisguised by close-cropped hair. He jerked to a halt, dropped his lower jaw and addressed the hapless Nigel.

'Ah . . . Ah, Lloyd. Making merry, I see.'

'Going to hell on an express train,' agreed Nigel moodily. 'Where were you at dinner time?'

Patiently he waited for the answer. It was a trait which, as much as any other, had branded Wilding with his nickname. He never spoke in a hurry, his voice was always a deep, flat monotone and, when he did speak there was always an initial hesitation as if he had to try twice before he could speak at all.

'I . . . I've been taking some rubbings at the church. They have some fine old brasses there and I'm collecting them to send to someone in the States. I had dinner with the Vicar.'

God help the Vicar, thought Nigel but, after all, the Reverend shouldn't have

66

been too put out by his guest. His profession was one which advocated the suffering of fools and he was no doubt grateful at the opportunity to practice what he preached.

'I . . . I see that your wife is with you, Lloyd.'

'Maida, Norman and a friend. Come and meet them.' Nigel led the way to where the others occupied one of the tables. 'Ted, meet Robbie. Robbie, meet Ted.'

'Robbie?'

'Eric Wilding,' said Maida with a frown at Nigel. 'You ate his dinner this evening.'

'I didn't eat it, you mean,' corrected Ted. 'No man born of woman could have eaten that swill and not regretted it.' He rose and held out his hand to the new arrival. 'Glad to meet you. I understand that you are spending your vacation at the school with the others?'

'Yes.'

Robbie didn't volunteer and Ted didn't ask the reason why but he could guess. Nigel had made no secret of the fact that he and Maida were staying because they couldn't afford anything else. Norman also was saving his money but Ted felt that Robbie had a different reason. He gestured towards the chairs.

'Sit down and join us. Care for a drink?'

'Yes, thank you,' said Robbie sitting beside Maida in Ted's own chair. 'I'll have an orange juice, please.'

'Orange juice. Anything in it? Rum, scotch, vodka?'

'No, thank you. I never touch alcohol.'

'Never?'

'No. I don't believe in it.'

'I shouldn't let the landlord hear you say that,' said Ted drily. 'I don't think he would appreciate it. Still, have what you want, it's your stomach.' He grabbed Nigel by the arm and led him towards the bar. 'An odd character.'

'Robbie? Yes, he is rather.'

'The name suits him,' mused Ted thoughtfully. 'He's just like a robot. How does he fit in?'

'He doesn't.'

'No, I wouldn't think he did. Poor devil.'

'Poor devil?'

'Unlucky, then. It comes to the same thing. How would you like to be an outcast because of something that isn't your fault?'

'You and your talk of luck!' Nigel glanced to where the others were sitting, Robbie very close to Maida talking, he guessed about his rubbings or the ancient stonework of the local church. She looked distant and bored, far different to what she had when sitting with Ted at the bar but then, he thought bitterly, the talk would not have been on such uninteresting matters.

'Luck is the most potent force in the universe,' said Ted grandly then saw the expression on Nigel's face. 'Is something wrong?'

'No.'

'You surprise me. You look as if you'd just swallowed a bad oyster.'

'Well I haven't,' snapped Nigel shortly. 'What the hell are we waiting for? Let's get the drinks and join the others.'

He had been wrong. Robbie wasn't talking about brass rubbings or ancient architecture, he was talking, of all things, about fortune tellers.

'They should be stopped,' he said in his flat, serious way. 'They are frauds, the lot of them.'

'Oh I don't know.' Maida looked dubious. 'One told me once that I would get married before I was twenty-one and I was.'

'A five nines per cent probability prediction,' said Ted. He met her blank stare. 'Ninety-nine point nine nine nine,' he explained. 'That's as close as you can get to total certainty.'

'Well! Doesn't that prove something?'

'It only proves that you are an amazingly attractive woman. Did she predict anything else?'

'She said that I would have two children and marry a very rich and successful man.' The way she looked at him made Nigel inwardly squirm. In self defence he had to join the conversation.

'Well, she was wrong there.'

'Perhaps,' mused Ted. 'But there is still time. It could all come true.'

'Surely,' said Norman hastily, sensing

the atmosphere, 'no one takes such things seriously. It's all a bit of harmless fun. As Ted said, Maida, it was a safe prediction to say that you would get married but all the rest was just window-dressing to make you feel good.'

'I could have done without it,' she said acidly.

Norman coughed.

'You were talking about luck,' he said to Ted in a desperate effort to change the subject. 'You even promised us proof of what you claimed.'

'Did I?' Ted looked startled. He had been staring at Robbie with a peculiar fascination and Norman's abrupt statement had caught him unawares.

'You did. In the car on the way down.'

'I haven't forgotten.' Ted glanced around the bar. It was crowded and it was impossible to speak softly against the hum of noise. 'You don't believe in luck, do you?'

'Not what you call luck.'

'How about you, Maida?'

'I'm not sure. I suppose there is such a thing but isn't it rather like ghosts and things? I mean, isn't it all superstition?'

'That's what I say,' chimed in Nigel. Ted shrugged.

'There are none so blind,' he announced sonorously, 'as those that will not see. How about you, Robbie?'

'I don't know.' He thought about it for a while. 'I . . . I just don't know.'

'I just can't believe this!' Ted shook his head in amazement. 'Here you are, all intelligent people, and yet you deny the existence of something which affects every second of your lives. Why, the most uneducated peasant knows better than that. They believe in luck and do their best to make it work favourably for them. Yet you call the most potent force in the universe a mere figment of the imagination. Superstition, you say, and think you have solved a problem. Damn it, you're as bad as those idiots at the establishment! They laughed at me, actually laughed when I . . . ' He broke off and looked apprehensive. 'I, er, I shouldn't have said that.'

'Said what?' Nigel was getting a little tired of his friend's antics but Robbie, of all people, was impressed.

'Where do you work, Bain?'

'It's a secret,' said Ted solemnly. 'Government research, you know.'

'Rockets? Missiles? Atomic energy?' Robbie, when he wanted to know something, forged directly at it like a bulldozer.

'Quiet!' Ted glanced over his shoulder. Leaning forward he lowered his voice. 'I can trust you, I know, but don't let this go any further. I . . . ' He broke off as a man barged into their company.

'Ah, Wilding, I feared that I had missed you!'

He was a small, shrivelled man with a starched collar three sizes too large from which his scrawny neck rose like the withered stalk of a plant supporting the balding flower of his head. Weak eyes stared from behind thick bifocals and his clothes, twenty years out of fashion, hung from bony shoulders. A wide strap crossed his chest supporting the leather case of a portable tape recorder.

'Sorry that I'm late, my dear fellow,' he wheezed. 'I had trouble with the car. Are you ready to go?'

Robbie jerked to his feet and said his goodbyes.

'It's a fine night,' burbled the stranger as they eased their way through the crowd towards the door. 'The moon should be out soon and, with luck, we'll get a prime recording of the mating cry of the lesser glebe and, maybe, the call of the horned owl. I hope so. It would . . . '

'Bird watchers,' said Ted as the voices died away. 'Incredible.'

'Robbie is a man of many hobbies.' Norman relit his pipe and the scent of smouldering hay billowed over the table. 'That's probably why he came in here in the first place, to meet his friend.' He waved the match before throwing it to the floor. 'Now, Ted, about this business of luck, you were saying . . . '

'Not here!' Ted looked distastefully about the crowded bar. 'This is a serious subject and needs to be discussed in serious surroundings. Let's go back to the school where we can talk in comfort. I'll get us something to drink and meet you at the car.'

5

There was a bottle of scotch, another of gin, a third of sherry and one of vermouth. There was also a jug of water and an assortment of glasses. The whole display, neatly set out on the table in the common room, did much to enliven the drabness of the place but Nigel wondered what the Head would say if he found that the demon drink had entered the sacred precincts of the school. Not that he was against alcohol taken in moderation — if he was the one taking it, but he insisted on his staff being abstemious and the common room now had the appearance of a dissolute pub.

'Here's health!' Ted had acted as barman and had acted with a generous hand. Nigel stared at the half-tumbler of neat scotch shoved in his hand and quelled his instinctive protest. Shrugging he added a little water and relished the taste of the drink. Norman was not so reticent.

'Hey, steady on!' He reached for the bottle to tip back some of the contents of his glass.

'Leave it!' Ted removed the bottle from reach and sat down. 'This is a holiday so why not enjoy it? Health, Norman. Nigel. Maida.'

They drank.

'Let us,' said Ted, 'talk about luck.'

'We have,' grunted Norman. Ted ignored the interruption.

'Let us,' he continued, 'use an analogy. Let us, for a moment, think of the thing we call luck as being a cloud of fine iron fragments suspended in the air. Now, people walk among, breathe, eat and are influenced by these minute fragments. Sometimes, perhaps because of an oily skin, they collect more than their fair share and such people are favoured among their fellow men. These fragments are, of course, invisible to the people and they can only guess at their existence by the effect they have on those who, for one reason or another, manage to collect them. Are you with me?'

They were with him.

'Good. So now we have a lot of people living in an environment of which they are unaware but they do know that some among them, those who, for one reason or another collect iron particles, are more fortunate than others. The natural step then is for everyone to want to become favoured and so, inevitably, they try to find some means of attracting the minute fragments of iron.'

'They make iron-collectors,' said Norman. He lifted his glass and blinked when he found it empty. Ted thrust the bottle towards him.

'Help yourself. You too, Nigel. Maida?'

'I'm all right, thank you.'

'Have some more sherry anyway.' He poured himself a king-size gin and it. 'As you said, Norman,' he continued, 'they make themselves iron-collectors. But, of course, they don't really know for what they are looking. So they try anything and everything hoping they will hit on the secret. Maybe they have some small success, maybe not. Maybe they only think they have or, more likely, they just don't want to miss out on anything. So the iron-collectors become very fashionable. But one thing on which they all agree. Iron is real and can be attracted. Naturally, you can see the analogy.'

'Who couldn't?' grunted Nigel. 'Call your iron particles 'luck' and your iron-collectors 'lucky charms' and you have it.'

'Exactly. Now, to go one step further. Let us assume that some genius among these people discovers something which, quite literally, does attract iron. We would call it a magnet. Bingo! The perfect iron-collector.'

'The perfect lucky charm,' snorted Nigel. He helped himself to more scotch. 'All right, Ted, you don't have to spell it out for me. It's a nice concept but what have you proven? We don't live in a world in which iron particles are suspended like oxygen.'

'No, but — '

'If you are going to say that the principle is the same I shall scream. As an analogy it may be good enough for kids and the feeble-minded but it's as full of holes as swiss cheese. Assuming that what you've said is so, and never mind arguing about the terminology. What happens when all the iron, luck, whatever you call it, has been attracted, collected, piled into sacks? No more luck?'

'No, of course not. Damn it, Nigel, don't take me so literally!'

'All right then, let us assume that there is an inexhaustible supply of luck. Now, assume that everyone has one of your marvellous collectors or super luck charms. What then?'

'They would cancel out,' said Norman from behind a cloud of smoke. 'Right, Ted?'

'Wrong.' Deliberately he mixed himself another drink, this time twice as large as the other. 'You forget,' he said deliberately. 'There are two kinds of luck.'

'Good and bad,' agreed Nigel, and then became very thoughtful. Maida stirred restlessly.

'If you are going to talk nonsense all night long then I'm going to bed,' she announced. She looked at Nigel as if expecting him to spring to his feet, then at the others as if waiting for them to immediately change the subject. Both times she was disappointed and, with a distinct chill, she swept from the room. Nigel hardly saw her go. His mind was busy with a new concept.

Ted, he knew, was no fool despite his warped sense of humour and he had flogged the subject of luck long past the point where it was amusing. Therefore he must have a reason for his actions, some private theory, perhaps, or a personal interest to which he hoped to gain converts. Curiosity, if nothing else, prompted Nigel to keep to the subject.

Ted needed little encouragement.

'You all know of Maxwell's Demon,' he said. 'It is a little creature of fantasy but let's assume that it's real. Now, we have a container of water divided down the centre with a sheet of material which contains a small hole. All the molecules in that water are in motion but not all at the same velocity and . . . ' He gulped down the last of his drink and poured another. 'Hell, just lets say that half of the molecules are hot and the other half cold but, because they are all mixed, the water has an even temperature. Now, if there were such a thing as Maxwell's Demon and if it squatted by the little hole and allowed only hot molecules into one half and kept the cold in the other, what would happen?'

'A miracle,' said Norman drily. 'Half the water would boil and the other half freeze.' He reached for the scotch. 'May I?'

'Help yourself, you too, Nigel.' Ted laved his throat with more gin and vermouth. He was a man who obviously believed in setting an example. 'Now, taking that as an analogy we can make a reasonable assumption that . . . '

It was logical, Nigel had to admit that. As Ted's voice droned on, rising at times as if he were a salesman hitting his pitch, dropping at others to stress a point, always appealing to cold logic and trained observation, he began to weave his own, peculiar kind of spell. The drinks helped, of course, Nigel admitted that, but like any man who has imbibed too deeply he refused to admit that he was in any way affected by the alcohol.

Luck was real. Luck was the selection of probabilities and was of two kinds. Favourable selections resulted in good luck, unfavourable in bad. Everyone born was subject to the influence of this mysterious, unknown but obviously real force. The world, no, the universe swam and was surrounded by intangible energies of which man had, at present, only the vaguest notions. Electricity was such a force, unknown to the ancients but now harnessed to be an obedient servant. Magnetism, gravitation, the whole electro-magnetic spectrum, all once-unsuspected natural forces, now known for the realities they were.

And so, why not luck?

Why not indeed?

And, once the possibility of luck being an actual force had been recognized, the next step was obvious.

'A machine!' Nigel choked over his drink. 'You're crazy!'

'Am I crazy?' Ted's voice was no longer the rather high-pitched, clearly enunciated stream of words that it had been. He blinked at the other member of the trio. 'Well, Norman, am I?'

Norman was nothing if not precise.

'That rather depends on what you call a machine,' he said carefully. His pipe had long gone out but a heap of burned matches revealed his refusal to accept the obvious. 'A magnet can be called a machine.'

'And so can a little brass image,' said Ted. 'Or an amulet, or a charm, or anything which is constructed with a particular operation in mind.' He reached automatically for the bottles. 'I like gin and vermouth,' he said to no one in particular. 'It gives me a lift, lets the bubbles loose in my head.'

From the level of the bottles his brain must have resembled a vat of champagne.

'Good luck charms are sold by the thousand, by the million!' He swayed a little on his chair and recovered his balance with an effort. 'Machines manufactured to control the elusive force of luck. They work too, if you can believe the testimonials but certainly they work for the promoters.' He sucked in his cheeks. 'Luck spelt money,' he said. 'Lots and lots of money.'

'A fraud.' Norman stared hard at the bowl of his pipe. Nigel nodded, wondering vaguely just where all the whisky had gone, the bottle was far from containing all it had done when they had first opened it.

'Money,' he said. 'I'd like a lot of money.'

They sat in silent, understanding and sympathetic agreement with that natural, human desire.

'If I had luck,' continued Nigel, 'I could be rich and then I could tell the Head just where to shove his job and school.'

It was a beautiful concept and one shared, at least, by Norman. They sat and thought about it for a long, relishing moment then Norman, more level-headed, gave a sigh.

'If I had luck I wouldn't be here,' he mourned. 'But I am and so I haven't.'

'We could make luck,' said Ted abruptly. His hair was dishevelled and, behind his spectacles, his eyes held a wild, reckless glow. 'We could make a machine which would give us all the luck we needed.'

Nigel sighed and Norman shook his head in an unmistakable gesture. It was never wise to try and turn dreams into reality.

'I mean it!' Ted lunged to his feet. 'I've got the stuff with me. You have a lab and small workshop here and we could build one tonight!'

It was a joke, of course, it had to be but, what with the drinks and the conversation, the others were ripe to follow any amusing idea. Nigel rose to his feet, swayed and clutched the table for support and then, when the room steadied, picked up the bottle.

'All right,' he said. 'Come on, Norman, let's make a luck machine.'

'Why not?' Even the phlegmatic master had been influenced by the conviviality of the evening. He joined the others as they staggered from the common room and into the passage outside. Ted turned, finger to his lips and gestured with the bottles he held one in each hand.

'Get the glasses,' he whispered. 'I've got to get something from my room but I'll meet you outside.' He gave a monstrous wink and weaved down the corridor. Norman leaned against a wall.

'Nice chap,' he murmured. 'Crazy but nice.' Liquid gurgled from the bottle in his hand. 'Odd!' He frowned at the label. 'Someone's taken the scotch.'

'That's sherry.'

'Is it?' More gurgling. 'So it is. Horrible stuff.'

'It would be.' Nigel thought about it for a moment. 'Different method of manufacture,' he said as if solving the three-body problem. 'That's why.'

'I suppose so.' Norman produced his pipe, aimed at his mouth and stabbed himself in the cheek. He was still trying to put it in its natural opening when Ted reappeared.

'Come on,' he urged. 'I've got the stuff.'

He had too. Beside the two bottles which he had tucked under one arm he held a large leather case. Odd tinklings came from it as Nigel led the way towards the school laboratory over which he held sway. As science master he was responsible for the place but, as a scientist, he held it in scorn and contempt. It was, he always considered, a relic of the past when a few test tubes, a couple of retorts and a bunsen burner together with a display of reagents constituted the layman's idea of an establishment dedicated to the pursuit of knowledge.

'Enter my domain!' He flung open the door, snapped on the lights and waved for the others to enter. Ted looked at the museum piece.

'Grim,' was his comment. 'Where's the skeleton?'

'We can't afford one. I've a life-sized drawing of a set of human bones, male, of course, for my biological classes.' Nigel waved to where a long, ugly roll rested on the wall. 'Other than that we have some fossils, pickled specimens which I think the Head bought at a junk shop, an incomplete set of lepidoptera and a plaster model of a cortex. We also have a star chart, a drawing of the solar system, a thirty-year old model of what we once thought the atom looked like and a few bits of metal to show the principles of heat expansion.'

'Still grim.' Ted set his case down on a scarred bench and carefully placed his bottles beside it. 'Glasses?'

Norman put down the glasses.

'Now,' said Ted after he had seen that everyone had a full glass. 'This stage is very important. Extra-sensory experiments have shown that the attitude of the experimenter can effect the result of the experiment. So, to get into the right frame of mind, we must all, at this moment and from now on, sincerely believe that what we are going to build will work.' He lifted his glass. 'There is no room,' he said sonorously, 'for doubt or despondency in this house. Skol!'

'What now?' asked Norman.

'We set to work.' Ted opened his case and revealed a jumbled mass of electronic equipment. Nigel recognized printed circuits, transistors, germanium diodes and a mass of other stuff all vaguely familiar but all incredibly minute. He said so and Ted chuckled.

'I'm an expert at sophistication. Give me time and the tools and I could fit boots on an ant.' The unsteadiness of his hands belied his claim but that unsteadiness matched the wavering of his body. 'A drink,' he muttered. 'We must have another drink.'

'Wha' for?' Norman looked as if, once he moved from the support of the bench, he would fall flat on his face.

'A libation.'

It seemed the perfect reason and they drank the libation, and then another and then things, for Nigel, began to get very hazy.

So very hazy that he never knew how he got into bed.

6

Seven navvies with seven sledgehammers beat with relentless determination on seven different segments of his skull. A high-powered searchlight was focused with fiendish accuracy on each quivering eyeball and a swarm of angry wasps had settled in his stomach.

Nigel groaned and wished he were dead.

'Wake up!'

Weakly he rolled from the shaft of sunlight blazing into his face and opened his eyes. Maida stood above him, a steaming cup in her hand, her expression totally devoid of sympathy.

'Come on now, Nigel! Wake up!'

'Wha — ' He stared wildly around him, at the dishevelled bed and his own, almost naked body. 'What happened?'

'You got disgustingly drunk.' She thrust the cup at him. 'Here! Drink this!'

Dutifully he gulped the tea then groped

for a cigarette. The smoke cut some of the fug from his mind and gassed the swarm of wasps lurking in his stomach. He looked down at himself, inglorious in socks, underpants and singlet. The bed looked as if it had been the scene of a life and death struggle. His clothes apparently had been flung to the four corners of the room. He winced as he felt a bruise.

'Who hit me?'

'You fell over a chair.' Irritably Maida shook her head. 'I've never seen anything so disgusting! You simply collapsed when I tried to get you to bed.'

'I did?'

'In your bed, of course,' she snapped, correctly reading his expression. 'You didn't think I wanted a drunken man spending the night with me, did you? If that's what was in your mind you made a big mistake.'

'It wasn't — ' he began, then had the sense to shut his mouth as memory returned. He had gone to Maida's room with a totally different object in mind and remembered the cold logic which had driven him to seek her out. But how could he tell her that he had wanted, not her, but some of her blood? 'I'm sorry I woke you,' he muttered.

'You didn't wake me, I was already awake. I've never heard such noise! Goodness knows what Mrs Beecham must think of your goings on. Banging and yelling as if you had all gone mad!'

That, of course, had been Norman's fault. Carried away by the project he had insisted that they leave nothing to chance and Ted had agreed. Nigel winced as he remembered the noise caused by their impromptu efforts at drum magic — the laboratory benches hadn't made very good drums. It had been just after that he'd had the idea that a little virgin's blood would help things along. Maida wasn't a virgin, of course, but she was the nearest thing available. He frowned, wondering why it had seemed so important and just how he'd hoped to get it. Cutting her throat would have been rather drastic.

'Come on now,' she snapped. 'Hurry and get washed and dressed. I don't want Mrs Beecham to think there is anything wrong.'

Maida, thought Nigel sourly as he staggered from the bed, was a supreme optimist.

It was late when he arrived at the common room. It had taken lots of cold water and more time than he had thought to get into some resemblance of human shape and the thought of food filled him with a heaving nausea. But there would be coffee, or what Mrs Beecham called coffee, and he knew that he had to keep up appearances.

The room was empty aside from Norman sitting with pale determination at the table. Nigel leaned against the wall and looked at the scattered remains of breakfast.

'Where're the others?'

'Maida and Robbie ate early and have gone out for a stroll. Ted's in the kitchen.' Norman automatically put his pipe in his mouth, lit it then hastily put it aside. 'You look rough.'

'I feel rough.' Nigel sat down with a groan, wondering, not for the first time, why men insisted on poisoning themselves. He looked up as Ted entered the room.

'Good morning!' Incredibly he looked bright and cheerful. He grinned as he looked at the others and set down the tray he was carrying. It held three glasses each half-full of a dark liquid in which, looking like a disembodied yellow eyeball, floated a raw egg. He passed out the glasses, lifted his own and stared at the two at the table. 'Come on, lads! Down the hatch!'

'What is it?' Nigel shuddered as he picked up his glass.

'A Bombay Oyster. Gulp it right down.' Ted set an example and, closing his eyes, Nigel followed suit. For one dreadful moment the egg stuck at his glottis and he opened bulging eyes as he forced it down. Then he waited, confident that he would very soon be violently ill.

'That's better!' Ted sighed with satisfaction as he sat down. 'I've talked with Alice and she's getting us something special to eat. Scrambled eggs and some well-done bacon with lots of toast and strong, black coffee.' He chuckled at the others. 'You certainly look as if you need it.'

That, thought Nigel, was the understatement of the century and, for a moment, he hated Ted with all the fury of a man with a hangover towards another man who should have felt the same but who obviously didn't. Then the Bombay Oyster worked its magic and he felt a little better. The food arrived, good food, and it helped even more. After his second cup of coffee he felt weak but normal.

'Well,' said Ted. 'We did it.'

'Did what?' Nigel lit a cigarette. 'Made bloody fools of ourselves?'

'No. We made a major breakthrough in the realm of scientific discovery.' He held what seemed to be a wristwatch suspended from the fingers of his right hand. 'Here it is, gentlemen. The first scientifically constructed luck machine!'

He stared at their blank faces.

'What's the matter with you people? Can't you remember what we did last night?'

'I don't want to remember,' said Norman and, recalling how he had yelled and capered as he pounded at the benches, Nigel could understand Norman's reluctance. He would never have suspected that Dale had had such an active imagination. Then he remembered his own actions and shuddered.

'The joke's over, Ted. Let it lie.'

'Joke? Who was joking?' Ted glared at them with baffled bewilderment. 'We set out to do something last night and we did it. We built a luck machine and here it is.' He waved the thing in his hand towards them. 'Look at it! Go on, look!'

They looked. As a wristwatch it was an ugly, clumsy piece of work. The metal band was too wide and too thick, the movement was too big and too heavy and the dial was numbered, not in hours but in degrees.

'I'm proud of this,' said Ted. 'The band contains selected metals which generate a current by body heat. The machine itself is in the box and the dial is to register optimum power input.' He snapped open the back. 'Take a look inside.'

It was complex and that was all Nigel could say for it. The fine tracery of a printed circuit mingled with minute transistors and other items he did not recognize, but one thing was certain. They could never have built it last night or any other night. He said so and Ted looked uncomfortable.

'Well,' he admitted, 'we didn't exactly start from scratch. I've been working on miniaturized equipment at the establishment and managed to collect a few things. What we really did was to assemble it.'

'Why didn't you assemble it before?' Norman had recovered sufficiently to light his pipe and Nigel, after one whiff, wished that he hadn't. But it had been a shrewd question.

'I did,' said Ted surprisingly, 'a dozen times, but it didn't work.'

'So how do you know it works now?'

'I tested it.'

'You what!' Nigel gasped at the enormity of the statement and then firmly shook his head. 'No, Ted, this time you've gone too far. The whole thing doesn't make sense and it isn't even funny.'

'Who's trying to be funny!' Ted, Nigel realized with a start, was genuinely annoyed. 'Have you never tried to assemble something and failed a few times before succeeding? And that's when you knew just what you were after and how it should work when correctly put together. All right, now jerk your imagination from its coffin and use your brain instead of your conservative reflexes. How often do you think Marconi tried to assemble his radio? How many failures did Edison have with his gramophone? Did Baird build his television receiver the very first time? How the hell can you expect anything as complex as this to come all wrapped up in an illustrated do-it-yourself kit?'

'All right, Ted, I only — '

'You only didn't think, Nigel, I know!' Ted breathed deeply and, when he spoke again, his voice had come down from the ceiling. 'In many ways this is a psionic machine. It is something which is affected by the attitude of the user. If you are convinced that it won't work then it damn well won't. I — '

'Psionic machine?' Norman interrupted. 'Like dowsing rods?'

'Just like dowsing rods,' Ted agreed. 'You know that they are in actual, commercial use and yet scientists refuse to believe that they can work at all? And do you know why that is? Because no one can explain the theory of how they operate. Two people can take a pair of rods each, or use the same pair for that matter. One will make them work and discover hidden water pipes or buried streams. The other will get no reaction whatever and it's a level bet that the person who doesn't get the reaction doesn't believe they will work in the first place. Because he is convinced they cannot work — they don't work. Understand?'

He glared at them as they nodded.

'Right. Now this thing,' he gestured with the luck machine, 'is based on much the same principle. I found that out at the establishment.' He snorted at what seemed to be an unpleasant memory. 'Scientists! Some of them aren't fit to fill a kettle. The mental atmosphere of the place was hopeless. But last night was different. We all expected it to work and everything was favourable. I tell you that last night we were all inspired!'

'We were drunk,' reminded Nigel. Ted brushed aside the objection.

'Drunk, inspired, what's the difference? Instinct took over and we meshed our psyches in such harmonious conviction that success was assured. I made some slight modifications, I can't remember just what they were now, and put the thing together. I think I made the last connection as you went off for some blood, Nigel.'

'Forget that,' said Nigel. 'Please.'

'The drumming could have helped,' mused Ted. 'We shall never know.'

'Let's stick to the point,' said Norman hastily. 'You say it works?'

'Yes.'

'How can you be sure?'

'By experiment, how else?'

'How the hell can you experiment on a thing like that?' snapped Nigel. 'Do you feel it get warm or what?'

He was feeling a little annoyed and more than a little foolish. The traces of his hangover had left him more puritan and conservative than normal and he didn't want to be reminded of the nonsense of the previous night. Also he didn't trust his friend and knew that Ted had a warped and perverse sense of humour which he was just as likely to vent on those close to him as anyone else. It would be like him to make the most outrageous statements and then to privately laugh himself sick when others took them seriously.

'It alters random probabilities into favourable circumstances,' said Ted pompously. 'You can hardly expect me to put it into layman's language.'

'Never mind the language,' said Nigel sharply. 'Let's see the proof.'

'All right.' Ted held out the machine. 'Take it. Wear it. Wait for your luck to change.' He frowned at Nigel's hesitation. 'Come on, you want proof well, here it is. Test it for yourself.'

'If it's so good then why not use it yourself?' Nigel's sense of suspicion grew as he stared at his friend and he remembered the old adage about receiving gifts from gentlemen of Homeric descent. Ted wasn't a Greek but he was as wily as one and Nigel couldn't ever remember that he had been known for open-handed generosity.

'You are suspicious,' said Ted, 'and you

doubt that the machine will work. Well, Nigel, that's just about the best way to make certain that it won't work — for you, that is. How about you, Norman?'

'I'm suspicious too.' Norman poked the stem of his pipe at the machine. 'Why don't you wear it, Ted?'

'I have my reasons.' He met their quizzical stare with levelled eyes. 'All right, if you must have the truth, I'm a little scared of it. Luck can work both ways, remember? This thing should work in a positive way it should attract good luck, but I can't be certain of that and until I am I'm wary of it. The last thing I want in this world is to be the target for a load of bad luck.'

'A nice neat way out of an uncomfort-able situation,' sneered Nigel. 'Damn it, Ted, you almost had me believing you.'

'You mean he's joking?' Norman bit savagely on the stem of his pipe.

'Of course he's joking!' Nigel felt a mounting flush of anger at having been taken for a fool. 'It must have started last night when we were talking about Alice and it's gone on from there. He got us drunk, fed us a lot of double-talk and now wants us to believe that we've made a momentous discovery. Hell, he's done something like it before!'

'You wrong me,' said Ted quietly. He looked at the luck machine swinging from his fingers then at each man in turn. 'All right,' he said. 'You want no part of this but I'd still like to try an experiment. Will you allow it?'

'You mean will we shut up and let you make a fool of someone else?'

'You put it crudely, Nigel but, yes, will you back me up?'

'No!'

'What have you in mind?' Norman was interested but, thought Nigel savagely, he didn't know Ted as well as he did.

'I want to help someone,' said Ted blandly. 'What you think of the luck machine isn't important now, but it is still something of value. I want someone to get that value.'

'A load of bad luck?' Nigel was sarcastic. Ted ignored him.

'Mrs Beecham,' he said. 'I've spoken with her and she is a woman I would like to help. Maybe this will help her.' He gestured with the mechanism still hanging from his fingers.

'Psychologically?' Norman looked thoughtful as he stabbed at the bowl of his pipe. 'Now wait a minute,' he said as Nigel made to interrupt. 'I want to know what is in Ted's mind. If he wants to make a fool of the woman then I won't stand for it.' His eyes beneath their heavy brows, shot an enquiring look at the tall man. 'Well?'

'I want to test this machine,' said Ted. 'Oh, I know that you don't think it will work and, because of that, it won't work for you and so you can't test it. But let us take someone who knows nothing of what we've done. If they can be persuaded that it can help them then, of course, it can. My candidate is Mrs Beecham.'

'Why?'

'She has had bad luck. If this works she will start to have good luck.'

'Logical,' snapped Nigel, at last managing to get a word in. 'But how long are you going to wait to find out?' He waved towards the kitchen. 'She never leaves that place. She eats, lives and, as far as I know, sleeps in there. Are you going to join the staff to keep her under observation for the next ten years to find out if she's stopped scalding herself or whatever it is?'

'You've got a point there,' said Ted. He looked thoughtful.

'Anyway, she isn't the best prospect.' Nigel was losing his irritation in a rising tide of enthusiasm. 'If you want to test that thing you've got to find someone who has been unlucky all their life and then you should be able to spot an immediate difference — if it works, of course.'

'It will work,' said Ted with calm conviction. 'Who have you in mind?'

'Robbie.'

'Robbie!' breathed Ted. 'The man we met last night. Of course! He's the perfect specimen.'

'Now wait a minute,' interrupted Norman weakly, but he was outvoted, outnumbered and overwhelmed by the others. Robbie was to be the chosen man.

He came in an hour later together with Maida who looked a little strained after her walk with the mechanical fount of knowledge. No sooner had they entered the common room when Ted pounced and, though Nigel hated to admit it, it was a masterly performance.

The attack, at first, wasn't obvious. There was preliminary skirmishing, a welter of conversational gambits until, finally, Ted manoeuvred his victim into expressing his curiosity about his business.

'Oh, I'm with the Government,' said Ted casually. 'Secret work, you know, miniaturization and all that. Tedious but interesting in a way. Like this little thing.'

He produced the luck machine and launched on a description of what it was supposed to do. Never once did he make the mistake of calling it what it was. Luck was too banal a word for something so scientific and so esoteric. It 'created a flux of determined motion of random forces'. It also 'established a field of influence in which the Heisenburg Uncertainty Principle was channelled into predicted behaviour'. The psionic capability was 'an attunement to the cortexial vortex of subconscious impulse' and the overall pattern was 'the predetermination of favourable opposites'.

'We have discovered,' continued Ted confidentially, 'that all men are not alike. Some, perhaps because of faster reflexes, are more fortunate than others. To put a label on the phenomena we can say that of two men one will win and the other will lose.'

'Luck,' said Robbie suddenly. 'Some are luckier than others. Is that what that machine does?'

'I . . . ah, yes,' admitted Ted. He gave his victim a sharp, suspicious look as if he suspected that Robbie was pulling his leg or was an enemy agent who knew more than he should. 'It isn't a word I would have chosen,' he continued hastily. 'After all the Government isn't interested in the manufacture of lucky charms.' His careless laugh dismissed the notion that anyone of sense could have ever imagined it. 'But what we are after is some mechanism by which the survival-chances of pilots and astronauts can be increased. You have heard of accident prones, of course?'

Robbie, surprisingly, had.

'Well, as you know, they seem to create accidents or are the victims of accidents to an extent which makes it obvious that they, in some manner, harbour a detrimental force. This machine, if you like to coin an analogy, is an anti-accident prone device.' Again the careless laugh. 'After all, when you are dealing with rockets costing billions, it doesn't pay to ignore anything to safeguard your investment.'

Sitting behind the smoke screen of his cigarette, Nigel mentally ticked off Ted's progress. First the arousing of interest, then the establishment of himself as an authority, now the stamping of the luck machine with the seal of Government approval. The final step, the persuading of Robbie to help the Government in its research by agreeing to become a guinea-pig, moved into its final stages.

'Well . . . ' Robbie was doubtful. 'Well, Bain, I'm not sure that I can help you in this matter. After all I — '

'Are you afraid of danger?'

'It isn't that but — '

'Aren't you patriotic?' Ted managed to look suddenly perturbed. 'Of course, you are to be trusted? I mean, if the establishment knew that I had taken you into my confidence without a thorough security check I — '

'I don't think you need worry about that,' said Norman from behind his pipe. Nigel quickly added his own reassurances, half of his mind hoping that Robbie would refuse so that he could gloat over Ted's discomfiture, the other half praying that he would accept so that he could see what his friend would get up to next.

'Let us,' said Ted grandly, 'try one small and very simple experiment. We have yet to determine whether or not you would make a good subject for a delicate experiment of this kind. Please slip this machine on your wrist.'

Robbie gingerly took the luck machine and stared at it.

'The right wrist,' snapped Ted impatiently. 'No, not that way, turn the dial so that it is on the inside of the wrist close to the pulse. That's it.' He stared at the dial. 'See, the instrument is registering as it tunes itself to your central nervous system.'

It was true. Whatever was in the case was working. As Nigel, who had left his chair in order to see better, watched one of the hands moved slowly round to settle on a point of the graduated dial. Ted clucked his satisfaction.

'High,' he murmured. 'This certainly looks promising. Now to engage the instrument with your particular psyche.' He moved what would have been the winding knob of the watch if it had been a watch and the other needle moved to coincide with the first. 'Good. Now we wait for the fields to mesh and for the potential to build.'

'How long?'

Norman, like Nigel, was getting impatient. Maida, who knew nothing of what was going on, had left the room during Ted's initial introduction and was now conferring with the cook about lunch. Ted half-closed his eyes as if he were making an abstruse mental calculation.

'I think we are about ready,' he announced. 'Will you step over to the table please, Wilding.'

Robbie rose and jerked himself in the requested direction. Ted sat down and waved them all to follow his example. With great ceremony he took a pair of dice from his pocket and rested them on the wood before him.

'Luck,' he said solemnly, 'and I think we can now safely use the word, is, in its final essence, the selection of favourable probabilities. All gamblers believe in luck and they have good reason to do so. Let us, for the moment, imagine that we are gamblers.' Picking up the dice he rolled them between his palms.

'Just in case you think I am being facetious let me hasten to inform you that this very experiment has the approval of the Rhine Institute for the investigation of paraphysical phenomena. Now, a dice has six sides and therefore it has a six-to-one chance that any side will fall uppermost. If we were gambling on, say, the six winning then the luckiest of us would throw the most sixes. Agreed?'

It was too elementary for argument. Nigel, his interest mounting, leaned forward wondering what Ted was going to do next.

'Right,' he continued. 'Now, with two dice, the odds are increased. Each dice has six sides and the chances of throwing a double-six are thirty-six to one. I think we can all agree that, if any of us throws that number with a higher percentage than the odds allow, that person is 'luckier' than the others. It is important to this experiment that we all agree on this. Norman?'

'No doubt about it.'

'Good. Nigel?'

'It's obvious, isn't it?'

'I should think so. Wilding?'

'I don't believe in gambling,' said Robbie firmly.

'I'm not asking you to gamble,' snapped Ted, showing signs of strain. 'I'm asking you to agree to a mathematical formula. Do you agree that the odds on throwing a double-six are thirty-six to one?'

Robbie thought about it then nodded

like a badly-oiled robot.

'Good. Norman, will you please throw the dice.' Ted tossed the cubes across the table and they settled showing a double-four. Norman scooped them up in his big hand.

'I'm trying for double-six. Right?'

'Right.'

Norman frowned, rolled the dice and threw. He shook his head.

'Try again,' urged Ted. 'Try twice more.' He waited. 'No luck. Now you, Nigel.'

Three times the dice skittered over the table and three times Nigel failed to make the point.

'Nothing.' He pushed the dice towards Robbie. Ted hastily snatched them up.

'Me first!' He threw, threw and threw again with no better luck than the others. Sighing he picked up the dice then hesitated. 'Check the instrument, Wilding. Make certain that the hands coincide. They do? Good. Now you try.' He passed the dice towards Robbie's extended hand.

Nigel sighed and relaxed as he followed the move. He glanced towards Norman

113

wondering if he had spotted what he had but the other man gave no sign that he had seen Ted pick up the dice with one hand but pass them to Robbie with the other. The explanation was obvious. He had switched the dice and Nigel could guess why.

'Double-six,' said Ted as the dice came to rest. 'Well, that proves nothing by itself. Try again.'

'Double-six,' he repeated. 'Twice running. Try again.'

Robbie threw the same number twenty-three times in a row.

'That proves it!' Ted leaned back, rattling the dice in his hand. 'You have optimum affinity with the machine. By the field generated within that case, tuned as it is to your central nervous system and affecting the laws of probability as they determine your fate, you are in a unique position, Wilding! My congratulations!'

'Is that all?' Robbie jerked to his feet. 'Do you want this back now?' He fumbled with the machine on his wrist.

'No!' Ted lifted a restraining hand. 'Keep it. Wear it constantly. Enjoy the good luck it will bring you.' He gestured towards the window and the world outside. 'You are a fortunate man, Wilding, more fortunate than you can, at present, even guess. Go now and accept your heritage.'

'You,' said Nigel enviously after Robbie had obeyed the injunction with the excuse that he was going to the village, 'should have been an actor. I've never seen such ham in my life.'

'Did I do a good job?'

'You certainly sold him the idea,' said Nigel. 'What do you think, Norman?'

'I'm wondering what will happen to Robbie now. It's an interesting thing from a psychological point of view — is a man unlucky because he is convinced that the world is against him or is he unlucky because the world is against him. And, if the latter, how can something inanimate be opposed to something with conscious will?'

'Now wait a minute!' Nigel was startled. 'You don't really believe that the demonstration was genuine? Ted switched the dice.'

'That is a low accusation.'

'Well, didn't you?'

'Yes,' admitted the tall man. 'I did. But only in the interest of scientific advancement. I didn't think you'd spotted it.'

'A child could have spotted it. Right, Norman?'

'I guessed. It was the obvious thing. In fact it was the only explanation for the results we obtained.' Norman held out his hand. 'May I see the dice, Ted?'

'Help yourself.'

'Thank you.' Norman, pipe clenched between his teeth, thoughtfully rolled the cubes. 'These, I take it, are the loaded ones?' He tossed them on the table. Frowned when they came to rest and tried again without success. 'Could I see the others please?'

'Did I get them mixed?' Ted frowned as he passed across a second set of dice. They looked, to Nigel, exactly the same. 'That's odd. I was sure that . . . ' He shrugged. 'Oh, well, never mind.'

'Double-six,' murmured Norman as he threw the bones. His eyes widened as they came to rest. 'No? Well, this time perhaps.

116

No? Once more then. No?' He frowned at Ted as again he failed to make the point. 'The dice,' he said patiently. 'The loaded ones this time please. I'd like to examine them.'

'You've got them.'

'No. You've mixed them again.'

'I haven't!' Ted flung the second set onto the table. They fell showing a modest two. 'See?'

'He's switched them again.' Nigel rose to his feet and stood over his friend. 'All right, Ted, now just try to be serious for a moment. We know how you did it so it's no use you trying to mystify us. I want to see those dice so you may as well hand them over.'

'You've got them!' Ted read the disbelief in Nigel's eyes. 'I tell you they're on the table. You can search me if you like!'

Nigel searched him.

'No dice,' he reported to Norman. 'Both sets are on the table.'

'And neither set is loaded.' Norman gathered up all four cubes and rolled them over the smooth wood. None showed a six. 'Well, Ted?'

'I can't understand it!' He looked pale as if faced with something strange and a little horrible. 'I could have sworn that — ' He gulped. 'Look, I've got loaded dice, yes, but I must have taken the wrong pair. It's an easy thing to do but — ' He swallowed again and looked helplessly from one to the other. 'Can't you see what's happened? The luck machine really works! There's no other explanation!'

He rested his head in his hands and groaned.

There could be no doubting his sincerity.

7

Maida pulled the dress over her head, tugged it into position and carefully readjusted her hair. Nigel, watching from where he stood at the foot of the bed, almost danced with impatience.

'For Pete's sake hurry!' he stormed. 'Where do you hide our money?'

'I don't like all this rush!' Deliberately she touched up her lipstick. 'If we're going out for the day I like to have plenty of time to get ready. It isn't as if we go out all that often either.'

'Stop complaining and hurry up! Where's our money?'

'What do you want the money for?'

'To waste on wine, women and song!' Irritably he delved into her chest of drawers, flinging up a froth of lingerie as he probed for their savings. 'Where is it?'

'Nigel!' Maida had been a nurse and knew how to handle difficult patients. He staggered back as she threw him away

119

from her things and slumped on the bed as the edge caught him behind the knees. 'Now, calm down and tell me what all this is about.'

Nigel sighed and then, because there was no hope for it, did as she ordered. The reaction was exactly as he had feared.

'Gambling! You want to gamble away our savings on horses! Never on your life!'

'It isn't gambling.' He looked at his watch and yelped as he saw the time. 'Please, Maida, for once in your life trust me. Ted and Norman are waiting in the car. We've got to find Robbie and get to Rolton before the first race.' Urgently he sprang up and gripped her shoulders. 'Listen, dammit!' he yelled. 'I'm supposed to be the boss around here. Now get ready, get the money and come on!'

Sighing, as if humouring a backward child, she obeyed.

'The trouble is that we don't know where to find him,' said Ted as he sent the car roaring out of the gates. 'The village?'

'That might be the best place.' Norman, pipe in mouth, eyes narrowed as if he were a Viking directing a raid, nodded as if coming to a decision. 'The village first. He might be on the road but if he isn't we'll try the church.'

'If you ask me,' said Maida from where she sat with Nigel in the back seat, 'you're all mad. What do you want to badger poor Eric for?'

'We need him,' snapped Nigel. He had tried to explain once and now, as the car hummed down the narrow road, he tried again.

'He's got this machine Ted made. The machine makes him lucky. We want to hit while the iron is hot and the only way we can do that is to find him, take him over to Rolton where they have a betting shop and get him to put our money on a horse.' To him it was as simple as the fact that two and two made four. To Maida, with her woman's mind, it wasn't that simple at all.

'How do you know that he will win?'

'Because he can't help it. The luck machine will see to that.'

'You mean that Eric simply can't help being lucky? That he will win no matter what he tries?'

'I mean exactly that.'

'I see.'

Maida fell silent and became very thoughtful. Nigel, fuming with impatience, leaned forward over the front seat, staring as if by the very force of his glare he could materialize the wanted man.

'There he is!' He thrust forward an arm and neatly knocked the pipe from Norman's mouth. 'Standing under that tree! See?'

'False alarm.' Norman beat at his smouldering trousers. 'That isn't Robbie.'

'No.' Nigel slumped as they drove past, the stranger looking after the car as if it had been filled with lunatics. Ted, in his eagerness, had driven recklessly close.

'He's had a long start,' he said. 'We took too long talking about what we had to do.'

That wasn't quite the truth. Ted, with his native instinct for making the best of any situation, had immediately grasped the opportunities the discovery of the worth of the luck machine offered. It had been Nigel and Norman who had wasted time. First they had to again search the tall man for fear that he had hidden the loaded dice. Then they had examined his baggage and found the missing cubes. Only when thoroughly convinced had they been persuaded to join forces and hunt down their missing colleague.

'There!' Nigel lunged forward again and Norman swore as he grabbed his pipe. 'No. Wrong again. Blast the man! Why couldn't he have stayed at the school?'

That was unfair and Nigel knew it. Robbie seldom stayed at the school when he could avoid it, preferring his solitary wanderings to the company of the others. Not, as he had to admit, they had ever been very much company but, he had decided, all that was going to change. It was with this in mind he had insisted on the presence of Maida. The welcoming committee had to be total to be wholly effective and he did not lose sight of the fact that she was an attractive woman.

Ted slowed as they approached the village. Stark was hardly the place to shelter a hidden speed trap but the road was narrow and winding and he had no desire to either commit suicide or murder. He braked at the sight of a familiar figure striding ahead of them.

'There he is!'

'Good.' Nigel writhed on the back of the front seat. 'Well, what are you waiting for? Go and get him.'

The engine roared as Ted fed it power and they snarled down the street to halt with a squeal of brakes beside the stiff, mechanical figure. He looked at them with a flash of reflected light from his spectacles.

'Ah . . . Bain. We meet again, I see.'

'And a most opportune meeting it is too,' said Ted effusively. 'I've been looking for you.'

'Oh! Why?'

'A matter of scientific investigation, old chap. The machine, you know.' Ted glanced to where it hugged Robbie's thick wrist. 'Still co-ordinated?'

'Yes.' Robbie examined it. 'The hands are still together.'

'That's what I meant. Jump in now, we have work to do.'

'I . . . ' Robbie hesitated, his Adam's

apple bobbing in his throat. 'Well . . . I was going — '

'You're coming with us,' snapped Ted firmly. 'You happen to have valuable Government equipment on that wrist of yours and there is an experiment still to be finished. Get in now and I'll explain as we go.'

'Please, Eric, do come with us.' Maida's voice dripped honey and cream. 'I'm sure that I don't know what all this is about but I'd love your company. Please come.'

Meekly Robbie entered the car.

The journey to Rolton took thirty minutes. The explanation of why they were going to the town in the first place and what they intended to do when they got there took a little longer. Persuading Robbie that putting money on horses wasn't really gambling but was a scientific experiment utterly devoid of greed and without the slightest taint of moral sin took most of the time. Finding a parking place and fighting their way to the betting shop took almost as long as the actual journey for it was market day and the town was crowded. Finally, to Nigel's relief, they were ready to begin cashing in.

'Dark Prince in the two-thirty is running at thirty-to-one,' he said. 'Right, those odds are just about right.'

'Slow down,' hissed Ted. 'This is a scientific experiment, remember?' He glanced to where Robbie stood like a marionette among the punters intent on their papers, betting slips and computations. Norman, acting as guardian and moral persuader together with Maida as diversion, stood beside him.

'Now,' he said, 'let me see.' He frowned at the list of runners. 'Dark Prince is one of eighteen horses,' he muttered. 'A rank outsider — the odds will probably fall even more. Well, what can we lose? A pound on the nose, Nigel. But make certain that Robbie puts it on and knows what he is doing.'

Robbie proved awkward.

'I don't believe in gambling,' he insisted as Nigel steered him towards the counter. 'I've never gambled in my life.'

'Do it for me,' pleaded Nigel. He shoved a pen in Robbie's hand. 'Just write out the bet and hand it in.' He glanced agonizingly at the clock. 'Quick.'

'Where is the money?'

'Here!' Nigel peeled a note from the thin sheaf he had collected from the reluctant Maida. 'Now please hurry!'

Dark Prince lost.

'All right,' said Ted calmly. 'To be honest I didn't expect that it would win. You are asking a little too much of the machine. Now, if you will allow an expert to concentrate on the subject, I will arrange for the experiment to follow well-defined lines together with the normal controls one is accustomed to use in matters of this nature.'

'What?' Nigel blinked and then became aware of Robbie looming above them. 'Oh, I see. Very well then, Ted, run it as you would at the establishment.'

'Thank you. Now Robbie, if you will pay attention please?' He moved a little aside so that the chosen instrument could join him at his studies. 'The next race has four runners. Now, by all the ordinary laws of probability each horse has one chance in four of winning.

However, these odds are affected by the relative speeds, weights, experience and skill of the jockeys. The true odds are therefore given in these little figures here. You see? Angel is at even money, that means the experts consider that the animal has an even chance of winning. But Devil's Apprentice is shown at ten to one against. Now, all you have to do is to decide that Devil's Apprentice is going to win this particular race. The machine on your wrist will then so guide the probabilities that they will act in your favour and the chosen animal will win.'

'How?'

'That we do not know. Perhaps the other three horses will each trip and fall, or develop some minor ailment, or suffer wind, glanders, cramp or simple laziness. That is what we are here to find out. Now, write out the bet — so, and put five pounds to win — so.'

'I can't,' said Robbie. 'I haven't any money.'

'Nigel!'

'Why me?'

'Don't argue. Give Wilding the five pounds.' Ted waited as the money was handed over. 'Now put on the bet, Wilding and remember, you sincerely want your choice to win.' He dabbed at his moist forehead as Robbie moved to join the queue at the counter. 'This,' he said feelingly, 'is earning money the hard way.'

'Talking of money,' said Nigel sharply. 'Am I supposed to collect all the winnings?'

'We share what we get.'

'Then we share what we put down.' Nigel held out his hand. 'If I'm to be the provider then give me something to provide. Norman! Come on and join the kitty.'

'Oh ye of little faith,' murmured Ted as he produced his wallet. 'Still, as we can't lose it's as good as money in the bank.'

He was a prophet. Devil's Apprentice romped home at the stated odds. For their five pounds they had won fifty. Gleefully they planned their next assault on the unsuspecting bookie.

'Jungle Juice,' suggested Nigel happily.

'A rank outsider at twenties. Fifty on that will net us a cool thousand.'

'Then Slime.' Norman was not to be left out. 'A hundred-to-eight makes near enough twelve thousand.'

'Then the lot on Harry's Boy. Only sevens but who's getting greedy.'

'That makes eighty-four thousand,' burbled Norman. 'Put it all on Criminal Folly at fives and we're made!' He sighed and shook his head. 'It just can't be true. There must be a snag somewhere.'

There was. Jungle Juice came fourth in a field of thirteen and sadly they watched their hopes dwindle. Ted, running a hand through his hair, swore in a manner unfit for the presence of women and glared at the list of runners as if he hated the very paper and ink composing their names.

'You're too damn greedy,' he snapped. 'You're throwing a spanner in the works. Why don't you all just leave this to me.'

'We were only trying to help.'

'I know, Nigel, but the very emanations of your mean little mind are disturbing the results of what, after all, is a very delicate experiment. It isn't what we want

130

that matters, it's what Robbie wants and he doesn't like gambling and has no desire to ruin the bookie. Money, to him, is probably nothing more than an abstract symbol. So the trick is to persuade him to co-operate, to make him want to alter the odds in his favour and to make him think of it as if he were a scientist wanting an experiment to turn out in a certain, predicted manner. Understand?'

'What do you want us to do?' asked Nigel glumly.

'Give me all the money you have. Let me do the selecting and advising.'

'Why do you want the money?' Nigel was stubborn. 'Why can't he just pick up the winnings and re-invest them on the next race.'

'Because that will make it a sordid monetary transaction,' snapped Ted impatiently. 'It will be hard enough to get him to co-operate without loading the dice against us unless we have to. Now, pass over the cash. We'll collect after the races and not before.'

'Can't you pick some accumulators?' Norman had more sense than Nigel and made the suggestion as he emptied his wallet.

'I'll think about it,' promised Ted. 'But this is a tricky business. We don't know if the force generated by the luck machine is progressive or not. If it is then Robbie will get luckier and luckier. If not then the energy may cut off at any time and leave him as he was before. Or, though it may not be likely, it may swing into reverse in which case God help him. In any case I want to make money not chance losing the lot through greed. Well, Nigel, what are you waiting for? The money.'

'All of it?'

'Every penny.' He scowled at what Nigel passed over. 'Is that all?'

'The lot.'

'Right, now go and keep quiet while I consult with Robbie on how best this experiment should be run.'

It was, for Nigel, a nerve-racking period of time. He could see Ted and Robbie, heads close together as they consulted the list of runners and then Robbie, with slow deliberation, moved sedately towards the counter the written bet in one hand and a wad of cash in the other. Impulsively he stepped towards Ted to find out which horses had been backed but Norman caught his arm.

'Don't.'

'I only want to find out which horses to cheer home to victory.'

'I know, but don't do it.' Norman puffed with a slow deliberation and a man standing beside him, sniffed, scowled and pointedly moved away. 'Ted's right in what he said. This is a tricky business and you could easily upset it. The best thing we could do is to go off and have a drink somewhere. As it's market day the pubs will be open. Come on.'

'Maida?'

'She had better come too.' Norman thrust his way to the street outside, the others in tow. 'What time is the last race?'

'Five-thirty.'

'Good enough. We'll kill time until then.'

Time, as Nigel discovered, was not an easy thing to kill. Especially when, as they discovered, they only had enough small change to buy a couple of drinks each.

Maida, who had held out of the betting syndicate, had a few pounds but firmly announced that, as they were all going to make so much money, she intended spending it on some personal fripperies of an intimate nature and could well do without masculine company while she selected them. She would meet them, she announced, outside of the betting shop at half-past five and to stay out of trouble until then.

Trouble, in this case, consisted of a couple of pints of cider, the cheapest thing the pub offered for sale, and gloomily Nigel discovered that he was down to his last cigarette.

'Life,' he said feelingly as he lit the solitary butt, 'is hell.'

'That rather depends on what you hoped for from life,' mused Norman philosophically. 'If you just wanted a bed, food and protection from the elements then you've really nothing to complain about.'

'Have you?'

'No, not really.' Norman toyed with his pipe as he thought about it. 'I could do with a lot more money but then, who couldn't? I suppose the best thing would just to be satisfied with what comes your way and to stop peering over the garden fence.'

'As a philosophy for living,' said Nigel, 'it stinks. Man is not an animal to be content with simple fodder and a stall in which to pass his days. He is gifted, or cursed, with an active imagination and is always conscious of the things he has to do without. Money, in this society, can provide those things.' He lifted his remaining drop of cider. 'Here's to money!'

Silently Norman echoed the toast.

Five o'clock came and Nigel lost his patience.

'Come on,' he said rising to his feet. 'I just can't sit here any longer. Let's walk about or something the strain is killing me.'

Norman didn't argue. He too, from the way he bit the stem of his pipe, stuffed it with reeking mixtures and used matches as if he had shares in the match company, was feeling the strain. Together they thrust themselves from the pub and into the narrow, crowded streets of the busy town.

'I'm going to buy a car,' mused Nigel as he stepped from beneath the wheels of a hooting monster. 'The biggest, flashiest, most ornate damn thing made and I'm going to drive it up to the school and see the Head and . . .'

'You'll be in a coffin if you don't watch out!'

Norman dragged him from the stream of traffic. 'Let's go and look around.'

They looked at the shops. They looked at books and baby-clothes, junk and jewellery, cheap glass and coated silver-ware, at all the stalls in the market and then, when the church clock chimed the long-awaited hour, they thrust themselves towards the betting shop.

'Something's wrong,' said Norman as they came in sight of their El Dorado. 'There's been an accident.'

'Probably some poor mug done his lot,' said Nigel with the callous indifference of a certain winner. He pressed close to the edge of the crowd assembled in the street outside of the establishment of Frank T.

Lomas Esq. Licenced Betting Office and craned forward.

'Steady on, back there!' yelped a man. His voice was echoed deeper in the crowd.

'Get back there! Give him air!'

'Maida!' Nigel flung himself forward as he recognized a familiar figure. Shoving, pushing, Norman at his side, he penetrated the ring of curious onlookers. 'Maida! Are you all right?'

She was all right. Pale, harassed, with a huge box under one arm, she was unhurt and more embarrassed than anything else.

The object of her embarrassment leaned against the wall beside her. Of Robbie there was no sign.

'Ted!' Nigel grabbed his friend by the arm. 'Ted! What's wrong?'

'Started screaming, 'e did,' said a cloth-capped man standing nearby. 'Started yelling and a bangin' 'is 'and on the wall. Dreadful to see it was.'

'Ah, taken with a fit, I reckon.'

'Some goes that way,' chimed in a third man with a knowing air. 'Right as rain one minute, the next . . . ' He tapped a finger significantly towards his skull.

'Nigel! Norman! Thank goodness you've arrived!' Maida glanced distastefully at her companion. 'He must be mad!'

'Where's Robbie?'

'I don't know. Ted was alone as I walked towards him. Suddenly, for no reason at all, he began raving like a lunatic.' She craned her neck over the curious watchers. 'Can't we get him away from here before the police arrive?'

It was good advice and Nigel followed it. Grabbing Ted he half-carried him along the road, the crowd, reluctant to see the end of their simple pleasure, trailing along behind.

'Let's get him into a pub,' suggested Norman. 'They won't follow us there.'

He was right. Rubicund farmers made a sympathetic space for the obvious invalid and Maida, after a savagely whispered consultation, reluctantly provided the money for a double-measure of medicinal brandy. Her reluctance irked Nigel for, as he said, it was a simple loan which would be repaid ten times over as soon as Ted had recovered from the shock undoubtedly caused by the enormity of their winnings.

But it didn't turn out quite like that at all.

'Robbie,' said Ted after he had drained the glass. 'May that man fry in Hell!'

'What happened?' Nigel, a cold hand clutching his heart, swallowed the lump threatening to choke him. 'Did we lose?'

'We won.'

'Then — ?'

'Robbie!' Ted shuddered and automatically lifted the empty glass to his lips. 'I used all my skill on our behalf,' he continued bitterly. 'I picked horses with a fair chance of winning, second and third favourites, lowish odds but relatively secure bets. I dumped all the cash on an accumulator — and we won.'

'How much?' Norman always believed in getting to the heart of the matter.

'About twelve hundred pounds.'

'Twelve hundred!' It wasn't twelve thousand or the near-million Nigel had hoped for but it was real money and he was a realist. 'That's . . . ' he frowned in rapt concentration. 'That's four hundred each.'

'Three hundred,' corrected Norman. 'You've forgotten Robbie.'

'Robbie doesn't believe in gambling,' reminded Nigel. 'He would be very upset if he thought we'd used him to make money that way. This, to him, was a clean, pure, dispassionate scientific experiment and we don't want to spoil his illusions.' He turned to Ted. 'Where's the cash?'

'There is no cash.'

'But — ?'

'Robbie handed back the ticket,' said Ted bitterly. 'He was holding it because I didn't want to risk his losing interest.'

'You fool.'

'All right, so I'm a fool, but how was I to know how he felt about collecting gambling winnings?' Ted beat his fist on the table. 'I had to sweat all the time to make him interested in what we were doing. Don't forget, for the luck machine to work it had to work for him, not us. He was wearing it, not us. If he didn't give a damn about winning or losing then the machine would have stayed neutral.'

'All right, I understand,' yelled Nigel. 'But what happened?'

'After the last race he asked me if I was satisfied with the results of the experiment. Of course, I said yes and he said good and that he was pleased that I was pleased. Then I made a mistake. I thought that he was subject to the same emotions as any other human. I thought that the actual sight of money would make him want more, lots more. I sent him over to collect our winnings. I saw him at the counter talking to the bookie. I saw them arguing then the man gave a shrug. I saw Robbie leave the counter. I asked him where was the cash and do you know what he told me?'

'I can guess,' said Norman sickly. 'I can guess.'

'He told me that the man had pointed out that he had been gambling and so, naturally, he couldn't dream of taking the money. He didn't think that I would mind as, so I'd explained to him, all I was interested in was the results of an experiment. So he told the bookie to keep the money.'

Nigel made a choking sound.

'Couldn't you have tried to get it back?' asked Norman.

'Have you ever,' said Ted carefully, 'tried to get money from a bookie who sees no reason why he should pay you? I told them that Robbie was playing a joke. I told them that he was insane and that I was his keeper. I said that he had stolen the ticket from me. I said . . . I said . . . I said . . . ' He gulped, unconscious of the startled stares of the inhabitants of the pub and of the burly landlord moving towards him. 'They threw me out,' he screamed. 'Threw me into the street!'

Then the landlord reached him and history repeated itself.

8

The Reverend Kenneth Wainwright carefully rolled the end of a cheroot in his mouth and struck a match on a homily advocating charity.

'I, ah, I'm not quite sure my dear Lloyd that I am fully aware of what you require. If you could, perhaps, be a little more explicit?'

Nigel wasn't quite sure what he was after himself but Ted had insisted that he visit the Vicar and Ted, in his present state of mind, was not a man to be argued with. He leaned back in the chair the Reverend had provided and glanced around the comfortable, book-lined study. The Vicar, he thought, had much in common with the Head. Both, obviously, loved their comfort and both were consummate actors. Or, perhaps, that was being unfair. Both had, in modern parlance, the requisite image for the positions they held. It sounded much nicer put that way.

'Well, my dear fellow?' Wainwright was enjoying his cheroot and managed to convey the impression that he would enjoy it even more if he were left alone to smoke it in peace.

'It's about Robbie,' blurted Nigel.

'Robbie?'

'Wilding, Eric Wilding.'

'Is he a parishioner?'

'He teaches at St Elmers. He is a colleague. I believe you know him quite well.'

'Oh, that Wilding, the authority on medieval brasses and the expert on the influence of the Saracens on the Crusaders domestic habits.' Smoke rolled over the wide, carefully worn desk as the Vicar nodded his enthusiasm. 'So you are his colleague. May I ask, my dear fellow, why I have not had the pleasure of seeing you at service?'

'Different denomination,' said Nigel shortly. 'Do you know Robbie . . . Eric very well?'

'I think I may make that claim.'

'Good.' Nigel hesitated, inwardly cursing Ted for having sent him on this mission and wondering just how to state his errand. Wainwright gave him a natural opening.

'Is anything wrong? Is he ill?'

'I'm not sure.' Nigel gave a deep sigh. 'Frankly, Vicar, I'm worried about Eric. He is not . . . well, he is not what I would call wholly normal.'

'Indeed!'

'Nothing like that,' said Nigel hastily, recognizing the Vicar's alarm. 'The boys are quite safe. No, it is in a totally different direction that his slight . . . abnormality reveals itself.' He leaned across the desk. 'May I speak in confidence?'

'Please do, my dear fellow.' Wainwright, Nigel guessed, was as eager to hear a juicy bit of scandal as anyone else in the world. He hoped that he wouldn't be disappointed.

'Incredible!' said the Vicar when Nigel had finished his account of what had happened. 'He actually gave back the money?'

'Every penny, stake money and all.'

'Amazing!'

'Immoral,' snapped Nigel. 'That stake

money wasn't his to begin with but that isn't important. The important thing is his state of mind on the matter. Is it genuine?'

'Is that what you came to see me about?'

'Yes.'

'I see.' Wainwright became engrossed with his cheroot wondering, perhaps, if he should throw Nigel out now or learn more of what was going on at the school. His curiosity won.

'Of course,' he continued, 'I can't really claim an intimate knowledge of Wilding but what you have told me is certainly in character.' He gave a casual laugh, a man-to-man chuckle. 'Even on our little fêtes, raffles, whist drives and bingo sessions, for the structure of the church and repairing the clock, you know, he has never participated even though you can hardly call such small endeavours gambling at all. No, I must admit that our friend is a man of the strongest moral fibre in that respect.'

'I see.' Nigel was not really surprised. He had known Robbie long enough to have guessed the answer but his mission was still not accomplished. Delicately he cleared his throat.

'Eric thinks highly of you, Vicar. I think it safe to say, without any desire to flatter, that you have a tremendous influence on him.'

'I do my best,' purred Wainwright.

'You have mentioned your little enterprises in the field of chance,' said Nigel, plunging on now with a desperate conviction that nothing he could do or say would make matters worse. 'To a purist, I suppose, such enterprises would be classified as gambling but . . . '

'Please!' Wainwright's lifted hand was a carbon copy of that so often used by the Head. They must, Nigel thought sourly, have both gone to the same school. 'Let me make this perfectly clear. I am against gambling in all its forms. It is a vile, immoral, sinful practice and can only be condemned. I do not condone gambling.'

'But the fêtes, raffles . . . '

'Harmless pastimes with a worthy object.'

'But you give prizes!'

'Small tokens of victory, nothing more.'

'The profits . . . '

'Go to a worthy cause.'

'And that,' snapped Nigel savagely, 'makes all the difference I suppose?'

'The ends can sometimes justify the means,' reported the Vicar blandly. 'Was there anything else?'

'Yes,' said Nigel grimly. 'There was.'

He wasn't skilled in theology and he lacked the basic grounding in causery but he did his best. It was, he could see by the Vicar's expression, a bad best and, when he had finished, he waited for the storm. It didn't keep him waiting.

'Monstrous!' The vicar was so shaken he ground out his cheroot, stabbing it into the ash tray as if it had been Nigel's eye. 'Incredible! The most disgusting suggestion that I have ever had the misfortune to hear. And, you, a Master of St Elmers! How can you not be ashamed?'

Nigel hung his head.

'To ask me, a Minister of God, to use my influence to lead a man into sin and temptation . . . ' Wainwright shuddered. 'Monstrous!'

'It isn't really gambling,' protested Nigel weakly.

'Of course it would be gambling . . . and you want me to use my influence to persuade him that it is both moral and right to wager sums of money in the hope of vast returns? Let me tell you, Lloyd, I'd rather see Wilding dead at my feet than lead him into such paths of unrighteousness!'

'But — '

'I have seen the terrible effects of the lust for gold,' stormed Wainwright. He was now, mentally at least, back in his pulpit. 'Widows squandering their last penny, men throwing the money which should provide food for their wives and children into the rapacious hands of the bookmakers, boys and girls, children even, gambling away their pennies, indifferent to the Devil which forever waits to snare the unwary. No! No a thousand times! Never will I be a party to such a sin!'

'You don't understand,' pleaded Nigel. 'It just seemed to me that, in this modern age, a little risk would be a good thing and . . . '

'Out!' Wainwright rose like one of the prophets of old. 'Out, you spawn of Satan!'

'Now wait a minute, Vicar . . . '

'Out I say!'

'But if you'd only listen for a second!'

'I have heard enough! My ears have been assailed and my soul shaken by the depths of human depravity to which they have been exposed. You have revealed yourself for the vileness that you are. You! I shudder to think of the risk those tender young souls run while in your care. Care!' His sarcastic laugh was like the bray of a mule. 'Drinking and gambling and smoking in the dormitories after lights out, no doubt. Wagering of pocket money on football pools and who is to stop them? You? No, not you. Boys follow the example of their elders and what an example! But they shall be saved. I shall see to it that they are saved.'

'Please,' said Nigel desperately. 'You don't understand. It isn't like that at all.' Wainwright wasn't listening.

'Out!' he stormed. 'Out before I forget

myself and lay hands of violence on your person!'

He was, despite his age, a big man. Nigel got out.

'Well?' Norman had waited outside in Ted's car and the interior reeked of the scent of his pipe. 'Any luck?'

'Lots of luck,' snarled Nigel. 'All bad.'

'Like that, eh?'

'Yes.' Savagely Nigel jerked open the door of the car and climbed inside immediately lowering the windows. 'The man's a nut,' he gritted. 'Worse than Robbie and that's saying something. Ted must have been insane to imagine we could get him working on our side.'

'Oh, I don't know,' mused Norman as he engaged the gears and sent the car moving forward. 'Most parsons are willing to get their hands on some cash. They always have a good use for it and most of them are tolerant enough not to worry too much where it comes from.'

'Maybe, but not the Reverend Wainwright.' Nigel glowered at the hedges streaming past. 'He's vindictive too. He's going to get the Head to give me the push. He says that I'm corrupting the boys.' He gave a mirthless chuckle. 'Corrupting! Hell, those little devils could give any adult a mile start in corruption and beat them with one leg tied behind their backs. Anyway, he's got it in for me now.'

'He'll get over it,' soothed Norman. 'Anyway, you might not have to worry if Ted's successful.'

'If.'

'He did it once,' reminded Norman. 'He could do it again. If he does our troubles are over.'

The thought was consoling and Nigel relaxed a little as the car hummed towards the school.

They heard Ted before they entered the laboratory. There was a crash followed by a stream of cursing and the sound of crunching metal. The door opened to reveal the tall, thin figure engaged in what seemed to be a war-dance. He glared at them as they entered.

'Well?'

'No luck.'

'You mean that the man wouldn't

152

co-operate?' Ted ran a hand through his dishevelled hair and left a black streak on his forehead. 'Did you offer to help him repair the roof, provide money for a new organ, offer to subsidize the Mother's Outing?'

'He wouldn't even listen to me,' snapped Nigel. He sat on the edge of one of the benches and stared curiously at the litter of parts over which Ted had been working. 'He doesn't believe in gambling and won't persuade Robbie that it is both morally right and essential to the welfare of his soul to indulge in the practice. Finish. End of one brilliant idea.'

'Damn it,' said Ted. Moodily he kicked at the thing on which he had been dancing. Norman stooped and picked it up, looking at it before placing it on the bench. It was battered and crushed but it had once looked like the machine which Robbie now wore about his wrist.

'No good?'

'Useless! It's just a heap of rubbish! It's no good at all!'

'What's the matter?' Nigel was anxious. With the prospect of no job, the certainty

153

of having no money and the fear of Maida's threat still in his mind he had reason to be anxious. 'Can't you build more of them?'

'No.'

'But why not? You've got the parts and what you've done once you can do again.'

'Can I?' Ted flung the soldering iron he had used across the room where it came to rest with a shattering tinkle of glass. 'How did we build the first one? Oh, I had some parts, I know that, and we put them together and we hit the jackpot. Right?'

'Right.'

'Good so far. Now tell me just how we put it together and exactly what we did at each step of the operation.'

'Don't you know?' Nigel stared at his friend with a sense of mounting horror. In the car it had seemed so simple and straightforward but now . . . 'Look,' he said urgently. 'Can you build another luck machine or can't you?'

'I don't know.'

'You don't know? Look, Ted, if this is another of your crazy jokes then, so help me, I'll beat your head in if they swing me for it!'

'Oh, shut up,' said Ted. He slumped on the edge of the bench, his thin face drawn and haggard. 'Don't you think I've been trying? I've done nothing else since we got back from Rolton. I'm worn out with trying but I can't get the bloody thing to work and I can't do that because I can't remember how we put the original together.'

'But — '

'I think I understand,' said Norman quietly. 'Think of an ordinary wristwatch, Nigel. Now say that you took it apart and put it together again but, somehow, the hands ran backwards. Would you know just what you had done from memory?'

'If I was a watchmaker, yes.'

'All right. Ted told us that all this was new and that he'd had more than one failure. Also we weren't wholly sober at the time. Maybe that had something to do with it.'

'We were drunk,' snapped Nigel. He was in no mood for the careful selection of harmless words. 'We were as stewed as newts. Ted offered a libation and prayed to the Gods of Luck. I did something — I forget what. You stripped and tried out some West Coast drum magic and I think that we repeated a Babylonian incantation of some sort.' He shook his head. 'We did a lot of things and, while we did them, Ted was putting the thing together.'

'Right.' Norman carefully examined the bowl of his pipe, a trick he had when coming to the heart of a matter. 'Now, of all what we did and what Ted did, what was useless and what, somehow, turned out to be essential? Until we know we can't hope to build another luck machine.'

'Uh,' said Nigel, shaken by the enormity of what success implied. 'Uh.'

'I've given the matter a great deal of thought,' said Ted sombrely. 'First, as you know, I didn't really think that the machine would work. When it did I thought that it was possibly the combination of unique circumstances and was best left alone. I mean, it worked on Robbie but there was a risk that it wouldn't work on anyone else. That was an academical question at the time because I thought we could cash in while the going was good. And, most important, there was the chance of a reverse effect, a sort of liberation of collected energy, which could be quite nasty.' He looked at their faces. 'Think of a rubber band,' he urged. 'Somehow it is stretched and stretched until, suddenly, it comes back . . . woof! I thought the luck machine might work on that basis and, after due consideration, I decided that it would be safer to leave it where it was.'

His listeners nodded with sympathetic understanding. Both men of science they realized that, at times, sacrifices had to be made but, being human, they naturally preferred that those sacrifices should be made by someone else. If anyone had to vanish in a puff of smoke then Robbie was the obvious choice.

Nigel voiced what was in their minds.

'How long until we can be sure the thing is safe?'

'I don't know,' admitted Ted. 'My personal opinion is that, if it doesn't backfire soon, then it isn't going to backfire at all.'

'Good for Robbie.' Norman, at least, didn't begrudge his colleague health and happiness. 'Where is he now, by the way? Does anyone know?'

'He's probably out bird-watching.' Ted stirred the assorted apparatus with the tip of a finger. 'Let's get our minds working on the main problem. I can't repeat the luck machine. We have to assume that there is only one of its kind in existence and that there is no likelihood of any more ever being made or discovered. At this moment it is around the wrist of a man who doesn't know what to do with it. Any suggestions?'

'Get it . . . ' Nigel broke off as he considered all the implications. 'Are you sure that there will be no danger of a backfire?'

'No. Paraphysical energy is a peculiar thing but, if those forces follow known laws then for every action there must be a reaction. Think of it as an electrical charge which could build and build until . . . ' Ted made an expressive gesture.

'Let's give it a couple more days,' urged

Nigel. 'Just to be sure.'

'He's had it too long as it is,' snapped Ted. He scooped up a handful of parts, swore as a sharp edge cut a finger and threw the whole mess into his suitcase. 'I don't know about you two but each time I think of how he gave away our money I want to take hold of his neck and squeeze it until his eyes pop out. Risk or no risk we've got to do something.'

'All right,' surrendered Nigel. 'We get it back.'

'Norman?'

'There isn't much else we can do. If Robbie won't work with us then there is no point in letting him keep the luck machine.'

'Good, I'm glad you agree.' Ted crossed the room and scowled out of the windows. It was dark outside, only a pale starlight illuming the night. Somewhere, out there, Robbie was hunting his bird calls.

He was having amazing success. Beside him the little man with the scrawny neck gurgled with delight as he adjusted his tape recorder.

'Wonderful!' he muttered. 'Absolutely wonderful! I have never known such good fortune before, my dear fellow. The tawny owl, the lesser crested glebe, even the nightjar and all in one evening. Incredible!'

Beside him, in the darkness, Robbie smiled in innocent enjoyment.

'We certainly seem to be having good fortune, Charles.'

'I have never known such luck.' Charles Grey couldn't get over it. He edged over to where Robbie crouched beneath a tree, slipped and sprawled over his friend just in time to receive an offering from above. 'Dear me!' He grabbed for his handkerchief. 'Would that be the owl again, my dear fellow?'

It was the owl. As an encore he gave a succession of hoots before gliding down on silent wings to where a half-grown rat had forgotten the first law of survival.

'There!' Charles trembled with eagerness. 'You see! You see!'

It was a sight not given to every bird watcher to see but, for some odd reason, the feathered wild life seemed to have lost their sense of incipient danger and acted as if no human was within miles. Finally, the tape full of exotic calls, the pair wended their cautious way towards the road. Robbie stepped mechanically forward then turned at a faint cry from his friend. Charles, following his companion, had stepped into a water-logged hole. Easily the big man hauled him out.

'Amazing!' Charles plied his handkerchief once more. His face was now mottled with white and black so that he looked like a native in war-paint. 'I saw you tread on that very spot, my dear fellow, and felt safe to follow as your weight is so much greater than mine. Yet the branch which bore your weight yielded beneath mine.' He wrung water from his ruined trousers. 'Dear me, still, it is one of the hazards we nature lovers must run. What?'

Robbie didn't answer. He was thinking, the fingers of his left hand wrapped around the peculiar object he wore on his right wrist.

9

Reclaiming the luck machine wasn't easy. Ted reported to the others in the common room the next morning, irritably waving aside the breakfast the cook provided and scowling at the contents of his cup.

'It's a good breakfast,' said Norman. 'Whatever you did to Alice has certainly improved her.'

'To hell with Alice.'

'Do you have to swear?' Maida, the embodiment of outraged dignity, rose from the table and swept towards the door. Nigel, his mouth full of marmaladed toast, called after her.

'Where are you going?'

'Away from this sink of profanity. When you *gentlemen* learn how to conduct yourselves before a lady I will rejoin you.'

'She was going anyway,' confided Nigel as the door banged after her. 'She always goes for a walk after breakfast, it keeps her in trim, but Lord, how she loves to make an exit.' He swallowed the last of his toast. 'Did you get it?'

'No.'

'No?'

'You heard what I said or are you deaf as well as stupid!' Ted glared at his friend and poured more coffee. 'He wouldn't give it to me.'

'Robbie wouldn't give you the luck machine?' Norman nodded as if he had expected as much. 'Did he give you a reason?'

'The best. I'd given him the thing with my blessing and he doesn't believe in returning gifts once accepted. God!' Ted slammed his hand down on the table. 'The things that man doesn't believe in!'

'Well,' said Nigel awkwardly, 'can't you make him give it to you?'

'How? Have you ever felt his muscles?'

'I didn't mean like that. Couldn't you tell him the Government wants it back?'

'I did. He just smiled and said he would be willing to co-operate in every way but I still haven't got the luck machine.' Ted scowled across the table. 'If you ask me he knows just how valuable it is.'

'Well,' said Norman philosophically, 'you did tell him what it would do and you proved to him that it would do it too. He can't be blamed for holding onto what he considers is his property.'

'Sure,' said Ted. 'I don't blame him. But just where does that leave us?'

It was a question which had no real answer but the prospect was horrifying. They had, somehow, made one of the most valuable machines known — but they couldn't repeat the discovery. They had made a device which attracted the beneficial forces commonly known as luck — and had given it away. The thought was enough to drive any sane man to gibbering lunacy.

Maida returned as they were discussing it. She carried a sheaf of envelopes in her hand and tossed one to Norman and two to Nigel. Both were bills. He looked curiously at the one remaining in her hand.

'For you?'

'For Eric. Do you know where he is?'

'Let me see that!' Ted rose like a

striking cobra and snatched the envelope from her and, 'Ah, ah, I thought so. It's from our old friend Frank T. Lomas and I wouldn't mind betting that I know what is inside.' He held it to the light and squinted at the silhouette of the contents.

'A cheque?' Nigel crowded closer, Norman at his side.

'It looks like it.'

'Give that back to me!' Maida was furious. 'How dare you take someone else's letter!'

'For the common good.' Ted handed back the letter. 'Maida, isn't today your birthday?'

'Of course not.'

'It is, you know. Today is your birthday and we are going to celebrate it, all of us. Now where is Robbie!'

They found him in the quad interested in the activities of a woodpecker and clustered around as he opened the letter a puzzled expression on his face. It contained, as Ted had thought, a cheque for twelve-hundred and ninety-eight pounds, the proceeds of their wager. The accompanying letter was very precise.

' . . . your name and address was given to us by your companion and verified by us by contact with the Rev Wainwright. We therefore have pleasure in enclosing a cheque for the full settlement of your transaction. As you can appreciate, and as much as we wish to conform with your will in the matter, our system of bookkeeping makes it impossible to retain the enclosed sum. However we are confident that should it prove an embarrasment to you there are many worthy charities to whom it could be given.

Thanking you for your custom and assuring you of our fullest attention . . . '

'My God!' said Nigel. 'A miracle!'

'Not a miracle.' Ted looked pointedly at the heavy band surrounding Robbie's wrist. 'Just good luck. It seems you can't even give it away.' He forced himself to smile. 'Well, well, this is good news, Eric. Shall we share out now?'

'Share?' The stiff features looked puzzled. 'I don't understand. Share what?'

'The money,' said Norman. 'What else?'

'But this isn't your money. I gave that away. This is a personal cheque sent to me.'

'You — !' Nigel broke off as Ted's hand clamped across his mouth. A sharp elbow in his ribs gave him the impression that the tall man wanted him to remain silent.

'Of course it is,' smiled Ted, 'and our congratulations on your good fortune. Didn't I promise that you would be lucky? Well, wasn't I correct?'

'Yes. Yes I have been rather fortunate lately. Did I tell you that we heard the tawny owl last night?'

'You mentioned it.'

'And the lesser crested glebe?'

'Yes, that too.'

'And . . . '

'Yes, yes I believe that you did. But you know, Wilding old man, we're in a bit of a spot and perhaps . . . ' His voice died to a confidential mutter as he led Robbie across the quadrangle leaving the others behind. Maida stared after them with a thoughtful pucker between her eyes.

'What,' she demanded, 'is Ted up to now?'

'I haven't the slightest idea,' said Nigel. The look she gave him was one of naked contempt.

'Something's going on,' she snapped. 'Everything's been upside down since Ted arrived and I don't like all this secrecy. I want to know what all this business is about.'

'What business?'

'Oh, you're hopeless!' She turned to Norman. 'You can tell me. What have you all managed to get Robbie mixed up in?'

Norman became very busy with his pipe.

'It's to do with that machine, isn't it? The thing you persuaded him to wear and that won't let him lose when he gambles.' She frowned as she thought about it. 'Or is it more than that? I remember now, Ted said something about a luck machine, Nigel! Has Robbie still got it?'

'Yes,' he snapped, goaded into indiscretion. 'He has and we want it back.'

'But you gave it to him,' she pointed out with simple female logic. 'You can't ask for it back.'

'We'll get it back somehow,' he

promised. 'Ted will see to that.'

'Ted! Always Ted! It's a pity you don't think for yourself instead of relying on that man. What good has he ever done you? If it wasn't for that trouble he talked you into we wouldn't be here now. Men! I'm sick of the lot of you!'

Angrily she stalked away and Nigel was just about to follow her when Ted rejoined them. He was smiling and, for the first time since the debacle at Rolton, seemed to have regained his good spirits.

'Well, that's settled. Robbie is sorry that the experiment cost us all our money so that we can't celebrate Maida's birthday but he, kind, considerate, gentle soul that he is, has come to the rescue. We are all going out, at his expense, to a night spot in Rolton.'

'Why?' said Norman before Nigel could speak.

'For good food, pleasant song and lashings of wine.' Ted winked. 'Especially lashings of wine. Get it?'

'No.' Nigel was sullen. 'Robbie doesn't drink.'

'So?'

'So if you think that you're going to get him drunk and steal the luck machine you want to think again. Robbie doesn't drink, I tell you.'

'Consciously, perhaps,' admitted Ted. 'But there are ways. There are ways. Anyway, the thing's all settled. We leave at seven. You'd better let Maida know, in fact you'd better tell her now before she says something out of place. Now, Norman, how about a second breakfast?'

The day passed, how Nigel didn't know, but at seven that evening a blue-chinned doorman ushered them into the dim-lit precincts of the Purple Dragon, a subterranean restaurant specializing in Chinese food, Continental wines and home-grown hostesses. There was also, Nigel noted, a cabaret which seemed to consist of the maximum exposure of female flesh with the minimum of artistic talent but on that, he was willing to suspend judgement. A pirate dressed as a waiter brought them menus of hand-painted silk lettered in gold. The prices could be shown in nothing less.

'This,' said Ted, 'is living.'

'It is?' Norman winced as he studied the menu. 'At these prices I can't afford to live. I can't even afford to sleep. Let's go somewhere else.'

'Why? Robbie's paying.'

'With our money,' Nigel grumbled.

'Maybe, but it's the only way we're going to get any of it,' pointed out Ted in a whisper. He raised his voice so as to include the rest of the party. 'Comfortable, Wilding? Maida?'

'Very nice, Bain,' said Robbie after his initial hesitation. 'It's like something from the Arabian Nights.'

'It's gorgeous,' said Maida. 'Simply gorgeous.'

They were both right. The management had, obviously, felt that the least they could give their patrons was something to look at, probably on the assumption that, of all they had to offer, it was the one thing on which they would, eventually, make the most profit. The decor, after all, was non-consumable. Expensive hand-painted tapestries hung against the walls, elaborate lanterns swung from the ceiling with smaller ones at each table. All were dim and threw a dusty, ruby light over the place aside from a patch of white at each table. The delicate odour of incense floated in the air and the subtle scents of good food rose from the chafing dishes on the tables of those already eating. Though early the place was half-full which meant either that it did a roaring trade or that, in Rolton, there was little choice of where to go.

Against such surroundings Maida looked truly lovely. She had taken care over her toilette and now, surrounded by her all-male escort, she seemed to be a Queen of Beauty. Looking at her Nigel found it hard to recognize the cold-voiced, hard-hearted woman who so consistently locked him from her room.

The thought was enough to drive him to drink and Ted was ready to fill that need.

'We'll have a couple of aperitifs first,' he decided. 'Sherry, Maida? Martini, Norman? Nigel? Something dry for you, Wilding?'

'I don't drink,' said Robbie firmly. 'I never touch it.'

'A tomato juice, then? Right?' Ted signalled to the waiter and beamed at them as the drinks were being fetched. When they arrived he lifted his own and made a toast.

'Happy birthday, Maida!'

'Happy birthday,' they dutifully chorused and Nigel felt like Judas as he swallowed his drink. He felt a little less like the infamous traitor after the second and didn't even think about it at the third. After all, he, in a way, was paying for the celebration.

'Excuse me a moment.' Ted rose and entered into an earnest discussion with the waiter. The man nodded and vanished to return, after a while, with a carafe of some clear liquid. Ted felt it, sipped a little and nodded his satisfaction. 'Water,' he said. 'I like a drink of water with my food but I hate this iced stuff they always give you. Now, Wilding, how about an aniseed drink?'

'Aniseed?'

'Yes. It's a harmless cordial they give to children in the south of France. You add water to it and it has a pleasant taste of aniseed. Perhaps, later, you would care to try it?'

'Is it intoxicating?'

'I have never found it so.' Ted smiled, a warm, understanding, man-to-man smile and Nigel wondered if he really hoped to get away with anything so raw. Pernod, though it did taste of aniseed, was hardly non-intoxicating. In fact it was stronger than scotch to those unused to it. He settled himself down to the enjoyment of seeing a master at work.

The food, chosen by Ted after due consultation with Maida and the frequent appeal to Robbie's knowledge was superb. He had spared no expense and the variety and quantity of the dishes assailed both eye and nose with tantalizing odours. Nigel was reaching for a small, harmless seeming dish of what he thought was relish when Ted casually held back his hand.

'Try some of this, Wilding.' He pushed forward the dish. 'I must warn you that it's rather hot. Do you like hot spices?'

Robbie, as Ted well knew from experience, lapped up pepper and mustard as if he had no taste buds.

They had the strawberries and kirsch which was, as Norman explained to Robbie, a thick, sweet sauce with a tantalizing flavour. The coffee was subtly different. It had a tinge of orange to it and a hint of something . . . Nigel shrugged and had another.

'Cointreau,' whispered Ted. 'High-powered orange liquor in the bottom of the cup before they pour in the coffee. I daren't try brandy, the taste is too strong.'

'Is it going to work?' Robbie, to Nigel's eye, remained as sober as ever.

'Something's got to give. He had quite a bit of vodka, the kirsch, now this stuff and he's ready for the pernod. Let's hope that he likes the taste of aniseed.'

He liked the taste of aniseed. Nigel watched in awed fascination as Robbie downed one pernod after the other, waiting for him to topple in alcoholic unconsciousness when he could be relieved of the luck machine. But, for some reason, he did not topple. Instead he seemed to become more alert than before. Maida, on the other hand, was more than a little high and verged on the edge of maudlin self-pity.

'It isn't fair,' she almost wept. 'I had a good life ahead of me, sister told me that I showed great promise and there was a young doctor . . . '

'Never mind, dear,' said Nigel hastily.

'Seduced,' she sobbed. 'Violated by a smooth-talking schoolteacher who lied his head off and . . . '

'Please!' Nigel felt himself grow hot under the collar as a few heads from nearby tables turned in their direction. 'Shut up, Maida!'

'Shut up! You heard him say that to me! To his wife! Shut up — that wasn't what he told me ten years ago when he ruined my life the dirty . . . '

The sudden clash of smitten brass drowned the rest of what she was trying to say. A huge gong to one side of the dance floor quivered to the beat of a padded mallet wielded by a synthetic coolie complete with false moustache, straw hat and wooden shoes. Twice more he punished the inoffensive metal and then bowed himself out with a servile stoop which hid his far from almond eyes.

The floor show began.

It was as Nigel had expected. In Soho it would have been cheap and tawdry. In Mayfair, because nothing can be cheap, tawdry or third rate in view of the prices charged, it would have been called exotic. In Rolton it was simply daring. Five girls scampered on the floor and writhed as if stung by a horde of bees. They were supposed to be doing, so Nigel learned from the menu, the Oriental Twist. The only thing Oriental about them as far as he could see was their hats — the management was undoubtedly taking care of the twisting part of the programme.

The music ended, the girls scuttled out, another took their place. This one was so obviously not an Oriental that she didn't even wear a coolie hat. In fact she wore hardly anything at all and what she did wear was strained to the limit.

'Hell,' breathed Norman in Nigel's ear. 'Are they real?'

It was a fair question and one which deserved an answer. After long and careful study Nigel gave his considered opinion.

'I should have to make a closer examination to be quite certain,' he said, 'but, yes, I think they must be real. They wouldn't move about like that if they weren't,' he pointed out, for some reason it seemed important to make things crystal clear. 'If you watch very closely you will see what I mean.'

'Disgusting,' said Maida. 'A filthy spectacle. What you men see in the sight of a naked woman I can't imagine.'

'She isn't naked,' said Ted regretfully.

'She might as well be, the hussy! Don't look, Eric.'

It was wasted advice. Robbie sat, lips parted in a stiff grin, his glass of pernod in his hand and his eyes like searchlights behind his thick spectacles. He shared, Nigel thought, the same hope of every man in the room and that was that the thin cords holding the flimsy dress together should break beneath the strain. It was a faint hope. Those cords were made of nylon tested to three hundred pounds and the material they supported weighed no more than a couple of ounces. He sighed then stiffened as the dancer gave a scream.

'They're real,' yelled Norman. 'Holy Cow! They're real!'

The cry came from the heart. Incredible, despite all logic and laws of chance, the tough retaining cord of the harness supporting the generous charms of the dancer had snapped and released their burden. A second scream followed the first as the G-string fluttered to the floor. Naked, looking a little like a whitewashed whale, the dancer hugged herself and then raced from the yells, catcalls, whistles and lewd suggestions from the male members of the sensitive and cultured audience.

'Well,' said Norman feelingly. 'Well!'

'Nice figure,' commented Ted dispassionately. 'A little on the pneumatic side but not bad.'

'I've seen worse,' said Nigel thoughtlessly, then cringed as he met the full impact of Maida's glare.

Robbie said nothing but sat, a fixed grin on his face, his head slowly revolving like the turret of a human-shaped tank.

10

At the next table sat a man and his companion. The man was a big, thick-set farmer with the scarred face of a boxer and shoulders to match. The woman, while no longer as young as she had been, was still attractive in a Junoesque kind of way and was proud of her shoulders and back and, to display them, wore a low-cut dress supported by a thin strap of material from the back of the neck.

Her shriek, as the material suddenly parted, made the scream of the dancer sound, in comparison, like the thin whisper of a flute to the full-throated roar of a factory siren.

Startled, Nigel twisted in his chair and stared at a generous expanse of naked flesh. He also stared into a face suffused with fury.

'You bloody swine,' yelled her escort. 'What the hell are you staring at?'

A second shriek saved Nigel the

necessity of answering what, on the face of it, was a stupid question. Hastily the man snatched up the drooping front of his wife's dress and looked wildly around as she swayed.

'She's fainting,' he shouted. 'Water, someone! Bring some water!'

Robbie, more practical, swung into action. A fainting woman needed water and, as far as he knew, the carafe standing beside Ted's elbow contained just that. Before either of the conspirators could move he had filled a tumbler half-full of the clear liquid and had passed it to the man.

'Here,' he urged. 'Give her this.'

'Thanks.'

Snatching the glass the man held it to his wife's mouth and poured half the contents down her throat. She had not just eaten chilli sauce. The sound she made as she spat the vodka into her husband's face was distressing to hear.

'You — ' His language, if not of the highest quality was at least colourful and richly laden with curt, four-letter Anglo-Saxon words. 'I suppose you think that's funny? Well, see if you like this!'

A sweep of a thick arm sent Nigel reeling to the floor, his clutching hands dragging the table down on top of him. Robbie stepped back as the man advanced, the pernod in the glass he still clutched in his hand arcing directly into his assailant's eyes. The man roared like a blinded bull, swung wildly, missed and tripped over the collapsed table and fell towards his own. The crack of his chin against the wood was drowned in the smash of glass, crockery and furnishings as he dragged it down with him sending a shower of dishes filled with succulent food high into the air. Maida screamed and Nigel, wondering if all this was a horrible nightmare, thrust aside what seemed to be a corpse and staggered upright.

'You've killed him!' shrieked the matron, her faint, and modesty forgotten in her rage. 'You hit him with a bottle! I saw you! Murderers!'

'Bottles is it!' A man had heard the cry and felt impelled to get in on the act. He snatched a bottle from a nearby table and flung it at the inoffensive Robbie who stooped as it left his hand. A man shouted in rage and pain as a pint of wine threw a quart of scalding soup over his face and neck as the missile came to an unhappy landing. His shout was echoed from another table.

'Hey, what do you think you're doing?' The owner of the bottle was justifiably annoyed. 'That was mine.'

'So what?'

'So take another one — right on the bonce!'

Both men had friends who eagerly plunged into the fray and within seconds the staid restaurant looked like a bear-pit.

Ted, wreathed in the remains of a Chinese dinner, brushed a bunch of soft noodles from his shoulder and jerked his head towards the door.

'Come on,' he urged. 'Let's get out of here.'

'Come on, Robbie.' Norman seized the unwitting cause of the trouble by the arm and headed for the great outdoors. Nigel, Maida firmly in his grasp, joined the exodus. Behind them the shrieking matron made the air hideous with noise.

'There they go,' she screamed. 'Escaping, the murderers! Police! Why don't they call the police?'

The manager had the same idea. He barred their path at the exit and spread wide his arms. He was a swarthy, blue-chinned Greek and he was not amused.

'Where you going? You a stay here untila the police they come. No one goes! No one!'

'There's a madwoman back there,' snapped Ted jerking his thumb towards the noise. 'We're getting out of here.'

'Nota so fast. You stay!'

'Not on your life. Come on, people!'

'I saida that you stay!' The manager grabbed at Ted who promptly thrust a sharp elbow into his protruding stomach. Wheezing the manager fell back yelling for help. 'Boys!'

There were two of them, both calm, both bulging with muscle, both quietly confident in their own strength. One of them casually punched Ted on the ear and the other, choosing Robbie because he was the largest and therefore the most likely to be troublesome, swung a leisurely left at his jaw.

One of the heavy lanterns chose that exact moment to fall on his head.

It was a heavy thing of wrought iron and painted glass and it fell with a crash which drowned out the noise from within the restaurant. The other tough stared down at his mate writhing like an impaled insect beneath the shattered mess, then yelled as a waving foot rapped his shin. Hopping and swearing he bumped into the manager and both joined the heap on the floor.

'Come on,' yelled Ted, one hand nursing his ear. 'What are you waiting for?'

They ran outside just as a police car turned the corner into the street.

'The gendarmes!' Nigel sagged weakly against a wall while Norman groaned at the prospect of indignities to come; the arrest, the appearance before the magistrate, the local newspapers licking their lips over the juicy scandal, the stern admonition from the Justice of the Peace, the fine, maybe even a prison sentence and, inevitably, the utter ruin of what remained of his career. Ted was made of sterner stuff.

'Good evening, officer,' he said brightly as a sergeant led a party of peace-makers towards the door of the restaurant. 'Bit of a shindig going on, what?'

'Have you just come from there, sir?'

'No, as a matter of fact we were just thinking of going inside.'

'I see.' The sergeant stared at them suspiciously for a moment then his face lightened as he saw Norman. 'Mr Dale, isn't it, sir? From St Elmers?'

'That's right.' Furiously Norman puffed at his pipe as if hoping to throw up a smoke-screen in which he could escape. The sergeant nodded.

'I thought I recognized you, sir. Are these your friends?'

'Yes.'

'I see.' The sergeant cocked an ear as a crash followed by a frenzied scream echoed from the Purple Dragon. 'It seems to be getting a little rough in there,' he said mildly. 'I shouldn't think you'd want to go inside with all that going on.'

'No,' said Ted. 'As a matter of fact I was thinking the same thing myself.' He began to move slowly from the restaurant. 'Goodnight, officer.'

'Goodnight, sir. Goodnight, Mr Dale.'

'Goodnight.'

'That,' said Ted as they passed out of earshot, 'was pretty close. A minute later and they would have seen us coming out.'

'What difference does it make?' Norman was bitter. 'He recognized me.'

'So what?' Ted could afford to be casual, he had nothing to lose. 'You don't think he's going to stand in the middle of the dance floor and tell everyone that he's just met someone he knows, do you? That copper's only got one thing in his mind, to smash up that riot and do it fast.' He stumbled and almost fell against a wall. Supporting himself with one hand he shook his head. 'Odd,' he said. 'That's odd.'

'What's odd?'

'The way I feel.' Ted shook his head again. 'I didn't drink all that much in there, did I?'

Norman, knowing Ted's capacity, assured him that he had hardly touched a drop. His statement seemed to reassure the tall man.

'It must be something I ate, then.' He drew a deep breath. 'Those strawberries and kirsch,' he decided. 'That must be it. I never did rave over strawberries.'

'The air will soon straighten you out,' said Norman. He felt a little unsteady himself and wondered how Robbie must be feeling. Like hell, he imagined, what with the unaccustomed liquor, the excitement and the cool night air. Still, that was all to the good. Once in the car he would probably pass out and they could strip the luck machine from his wrist and, when he woke, swear that he must have lost it somehow during the brawl.

Confidently he looked back at the unsuspecting victim who was following up with Nigel and Maida. He blinked, stared harder and grabbed Ted's arm.

'I don't believe it,' he muttered. 'Look at him, Ted! Stone-cold sober!'

'He can't be!'

'He is. Are you sure you fed him the right stuff?'

'Of course I'm sure.' Ted halted beside the car and narrowed his eyes as the others approached. 'Inertia,' he decided. 'He's operating on sheer inertia. Never having touched alcohol he doesn't know what the effects are and he is walking and moving on built-in conditioned reflexes. Wait until he stoops to get inside and he'll roll right over.'

For once the oracle was wrong. Robbie didn't roll over instead he sat as straight and as mechanical as ever behind the driver, politely moving into the corner as Maida sat beside him and somehow edging back as Nigel squeezed into the remainder of the rear seat. Norman hastily lit his pipe and sent clouds of smoke rolling towards the rear of the car. It was no time for half-measures.

'Feel all right, Wilding?'

'Yes, thank you.'

'Not sick or anything?'

'Not a bit.' Robbie frowned as if he felt the question held a deeper meaning. 'Why?'

191

'Oh, no particular reason. I just wondered. Rich food and all that.' He blew more smoke, ignoring Maida's hands as they sought to create a breeze to dispel the fumes. 'Head all right?'

'Yes, thank you. Quite all right.'

'Please, Norman!' Maida forced a pointed cough. 'Must you blow that horrible smoke all over us?'

'Sorry.' Norman slumped back into his seat and wondered at the alien chemistry of his colleague as Ted sent the car humming down the street. Something must have gone wrong, he decided and yet, the carafe had contained vodka and Robbie had certainly knocked back the pernods. It was, he decided philosophically, just another of life's mysteries.

Ted wasn't so philosophic. Glaring into the rear view mirror he met the bland stare of the man behind him and fumed at the other's undoubted sobriety. That sobriety was, in a sense, an insult, a blatant defiance of his craftily engineered scheme and the worst part about it was that he felt far from sober himself. It was almost, he thought savagely, as if Robbie, by some magic alchemy, had transferred the effects he should be feeling to himself.

It was a challenge and he rose to the occasion.

'Ted!' Maida screamed as the car lurched around a corner with a squeal of protest from the tyres and screamed again as he spun the wheel in a reverse direction. 'Ted! Be careful!'

'Sorry,' he lied. 'Nasty bend that.' He tightened his grip on the wheel. 'Watch it! Here's another!'

There wasn't but it didn't matter. From the back seat they could only see the unlit road in the glare of the headlights and, for all they knew, he was justified in sending the car in a series of violent curves which threw Maida first against her husband and then equally hard against Robbie.

'Ted! Please!'

'Sorry,' he lied again. Then jammed his foot on the brake.

'Rabbit,' he apologized. 'Nearly ran the poor thing over. Whoops! There's another.' The car lurched as he played with accelerator and brake then seemed to take-off as he hit a humped-back bridge. It couldn't, he thought gleefully, be very long now.

'Please!' Nigel leaned forward, his face ghastly in the green glow from the instrument panel. 'Please stop the car, Ted. I want to be sick.'

'Sick?' Ted flung the car in another savage double-curve. The whole point of the wild driving had been to unsettle the stomachs of those in the rear but Robbie, not Nigel, should have been the one affected.

'Please!' Nigel sounded desperate. 'Ted . . . I can't . . . '

Tyres squealed as Ted clamped on the brakes. A door swung open and distressing sounds came from the grass verge. Norman, his face strained, opened his own door.

'I think,' he said carefully, 'I'll go for a short walk.'

'I'll come with you.' Ted slid from beneath the wheel. 'Want to spend a penny, Maida?'

'No thank you,' she said primly.

'Robbie?'

'No. I'll just sit here until you get back.'

'The scheme,' said Norman, 'isn't going to work.' He glanced sidewise at Ted as they walked through the long grass at the side of the road. Behind them the car, headlights still blazing, illuminated the road to their rear. Beside it Nigel crouched in heaving misery careless of the nettles in which he stood.

'I don't understand it,' said Ted. He was puzzled. 'By all the laws of logic, science and human chemistry Robbie should have passed out long ago. The man must have a metal stomach!'

'It's odd,' agreed Norman.

'It's more than odd. Are you positive that he isn't a secret drinker?'

'If he was then how would I know it? If I did then it wouldn't be secret.'

'Don't get precise on me,' snapped Ted. 'You know what I mean.'

'I know, but I doubt it. Rumour gets around in small places and he'd have to get his supplies from somewhere, wouldn't he? No. I don't think he's ever touched a drop in his life.'

'Then it beats me,' sighed Ted. He

halted, looking back at the car. 'There's still hope,' he decided. 'Robbie is a freak but even his freakishness must have limits. Maybe it takes longer than normal for food to penetrate his stomach. Or maybe his metabolism is weird but that liquor must take effect soon. It's my guess he will suddenly keel over and, when he does, victory!'

'Maybe.' Norman wasn't such an optimist.

'I feel,' said Ted, 'that something strange and wonderful is going to happen tonight. It is in the air. A kind of magic. I can sense it in my blood. It is as if strange creatures of limitless intelligence were communing their deepest secrets and will reveal to us new and wondrous things of ineffable enchantment.'

'Are you all right?'

'Of course I'm all right.'

'You sound odd to me.'

'I feel odd. It was those strawberries. Don't you feel odd too?'

'No. Do you want me to drive?'

'Certainly not.'

'But — '

'Let us,' said Ted stiffly, 'return to the car.'

Nigel had reseated himself. He crouched, a pale and shrunken shape beside the fullsome softness of his wife looking a little, Ted thought, like the husband of the Black Widow spider who has just mated and waits humbly for death. Robbie, aside from a certain smugness revealed in the subtle upturning of the corners of his mouth, looked just the same as he always did.

'All right, Nigel?' Ted slammed the driver's door and trod on the clutch. 'Sure? Off we go then.'

He sent the car rocketing into the darkness.

Nigel groaned as the violent surge of acceleration threw him back against the upholstery but Ted was not being sadistic. He had thought of a plan which, in his state of euphoria, had all the pristine beauty of naked simplicity. It depended on the fact that Robbie would hardly vanish into his room the moment they arrived back at the school. They would assemble in the common room and talk, and inevitably, there would be coffee. Strong coffee. Coffee so strong and black that it would, perhaps, disguise the taste of the scotch resting at this very moment in his room.

It would, he hoped, be the straw to break Robbie's apparent immunity to alcohol.

Smiling to himself, already mentally engaged in the subtle conversation which would lead his unwitting victim to the slaughter, he was in no state to be fully conscious of what was before him and certainly in no state to be driving so fast through the night. Luck was with them, they met nothing on the road and soon they approached the school.

'Here we are,' said Ted. 'Home at last. Who would like a cup of coffee?'

'Yes, please,' said Maida.

'I'd like a cup,' said Robbie.

Ted grinned at the initial success of his plan and nudged Norman in the ribs.

'What — ?'

'You'd like some coffee, wouldn't you, Norman?'

'Uh? Well — '

'Of course you would. And you, Nigel?'

Nigel didn't want coffee. He wanted nothing more at the moment than to be allowed to crawl from the car and into bed where he could nurse the sickening heavings of his tormented stomach. In bed with, perhaps, someone sympathetic and understanding to ease his fevered brow. In the darkness his hand groped for that of Maida. He couldn't find her hand but he did find the smooth roundness of her thigh. He squeezed it, mentally sighing at pleasant memories, remembering when such an action on his part would have been met with bright-eyed approval and soft-voiced invitation.

'Don't paw me, Nigel,' she said sharply. 'You know I don't like it.'

'Now, now,' said Ted. 'No fighting back there. And no snogging, you two, you know how it upsets us bachelors.'

Gleefully he swung the car through the gates, roared across the quad and yelled as a car seemed to spring from the ground directly before him.

'What the — '

Desperately he wrenched at the wheel, knowing that he couldn't possibly avoid a collision. Maida screamed, her yell echoed by a shriek of protest from the tyres, and the headlights arced crazily across the sky. The car gave a peculiar, sidewise lurch and came to an abrupt halt. Norman, caught unawares, hurtled forward and slammed his head against the windscreen which, for some reason, didn't shatter. Nigel's stomach gave a tremendous heave and he grabbed desperately for his handkerchief. Maida shrieked again as she cushioned the full impact of Robbie's weight and Ted groaned as the steering wheel dug into his lower ribs.

Dazed, winded, hardly daring to believe that he was still alive, he became conscious of a voice.

It was a strong voice and it belonged to an irate man. It rose above the creak of cooling metal, the slammed door of the other car and the crunch of gravel beneath advancing feet. It grew louder as the owner approached and, to Nigel, it had a haunting, familiar quality.

The Reverend Kenneth Wainwright reached the car, jerked open the side door and stepped hastily back as the limp form of Norman rolled at his feet.

11

'And then what happened?' Norman sat up in bed, a purple bruise over one eye, his pipe held like a flag of non-surrender in his mouth. He was unshaven, haggard, the whites of his eyes stained a dingy yellow. Above the garish pyjamas the thick hair of his chest climbed towards his throat. He looked, thought Nigel absently, a little like an ape who was doing his best to appear human and almost immediately felt ashamed of the thought. Norman, at least, was his friend.

'Wainwright thought you were drunk and had passed out. In fact he thought we were all drunk aside from Robbie and he didn't choose his words in saying just what he thought of us. I can't say that I blame him, really. The inside of the car was a mess, I'd been ill, and the air reeked of booze. Ted, of course, had to argue.'

'He would,' said Norman. 'He is an

argumentative man.'

'He's a clot,' snapped Nigel. 'He got out of the car and promptly fell over — he said his legs were weak but, to the vicar, the reason was obvious. He called him an imp of Satan leading the godly, meaning Robbie, into paths of unrighteousness. He threatened him with anathema, physical violence and the weight of the law in that order.'

'The vicar,' mused Norman thoughtfully, 'must have been upset.'

'He'd almost been killed and he had a right to be. The way Ted drove last night was utter lunacy. Anyway, instead of being sensible he defied Wainwright, told him to go home and read his Bible and to pay special attention to the Lord's Prayer and the Sermon on the Mount. He also pointed out that, as the quad is private ground, he could go and stuff his law. Then he got sarcastic and said that the vicar should thank him for having brought the fact that we are all on this world for only a short while to his notice. He even suggested that, as the vicar must be confident that he would go to Heaven when he died, he should be grateful to anyone who sent him there. You can guess how Wainwright took that.'

'I can guess,' said Norman broodingly. 'And then?'

'We were all out of the car by then and I managed to push Maida between Ted and the vicar, I knew that he would never hit a woman. Anyway, he grabbed Robbie and headed for his own car. Before he left he warned us that we hadn't heard the last of this.'

'I bet we haven't.' Norman reached automatically for matches and lit his pipe. 'The Head will be delighted to hear how his resident staff conducted themselves during his absence. What was the vicar doing here, anyway?'

'He'd called for Robbie. He'd received some slides or something he wanted to show him. Ted was raging like a madman as they drove away, I think he had some plan or other which the vicar had spoiled. Anyway, we managed to carry you into the school and get you to bed. The doctor will be here soon.'

'The doctor?'

'Yes, I had to call him. He's with Maida now.'

He didn't describe the painful scene of a short while ago when Maida had insisted that she receive medical attention for her bruised ribs. In vain he had pointed out that the injury wasn't serious and that the fewer people who knew of the activities of the previous night the better. She had called him a heartless, callous swine and had pointed out that, as far as they knew, Norman had concussion, a splintered skull or a lacerated brain. In any case she had insisted that he summon Doctor West immediately.

The doctor was a member of the old school. He wore faded black thirty years out of date, a pearl-headed stick-pin in his tie, a pair of gold-rimmed pince-nez and smelt of damp, dust and iodine. He came bustling into the bedroom, his little black bag in his hand and the number five expression on his face. This was a jolly smile reflecting an air of supreme confidence and a mannish understanding of the foibles and weaknesses of the human race. Douglas West, Nigel suspected, had been listening to rumour.

'Well, well,' he boomed setting down the bag. 'Now what have we here? A bump on the head, what?'

'You could call it that,' agreed Norman. He winced as the doctor's fingers probed at his skull. 'I banged my head last night.'

'So I understand.'

'On the windscreen of a car. It was an accident.'

'Aren't they all, my dear fellow? There! Did that hurt?'

'Like hell.'

'Good. And that?'

'Like two hells.'

'Good. Good. We haven't lost our sense of humour I see. Well, I've seen worse after a hard game of rugger, much worse, but we'll make sure, shall we?' He dug an ophthalmoscope from the interior of his bag. 'Just rest back and look at the light. Um ... Um ... Once again please. Um ...'

'Is it bad?' Nigel's imagination, as always, had run away with him at the sight of medical instruments and the doctor's tone, which he had used from sheer habit, had made him expect the worst.

'Just a slight contusion,' said West, rising with an audible creak from his lumbar region. 'No fracture that I can see and nothing but the very slightest of concussions. Take things easy for a while,' he said to Norman. 'If the pain should get worse or you have continual headaches let me know and we'll arrange for an X-ray.' Throwing the ophthalmoscope back into his bag he produced a roll of sticky bandage and a bottle of antiseptic. 'I'll just put a dressing on this small cut while I'm here.'

'Don't bother.'

'Think nothing of it, my dear fellow. It's just an elementary . . . '

Nigel left the room as the doctor busied himself with his reluctant patient. The bandage, he suspected, would remain on Norman's head just as long as it took him to take it off after the doctor had gone but he wasn't concerned over that. He was worried about Maida.

She turned as he entered her room, a fascinating vision of creamy skin and frilly underwear. Both hands were behind her back and she was wincing as she tried to hook an intimate undergarment into place.

'Nigel! Thank goodness you've come. Hook me up.'

'Must I?' He rested possessive hands on her hips and nibbled her shoulder. 'Maida, you look wonderful!'

'I don't feel it. Are you going to hook me up or not?'

'Why didn't you get West to do it?' he said nastily. 'I bet that the old goat would have loved it.'

'He isn't an old goat and you don't ask a doctor to do things like that. In fact you should have been here while he examined me. Why weren't you?'

'I was with Norman.'

'How is he?'

'As I thought. Just a bump on the head and that's all. There's no more wrong with him than there is with you. We didn't need the doctor at all.'

'That,' she said, frowning a little as he

hooked her up, 'is where you laymen make me sick. If you'd ever worked in a hospital as I have you'd know how important it is to be sure. A blow on the head could have serious results. He could develop a lesion or a brain tumour or . . .'

'All right,' he surrendered, 'don't blind me with your superior knowledge. Anyway, there's nothing wrong with him and there's nothing wrong with you.'

'I,' she said stiffly, 'have multiple lesions of the subcutaneous tissue and extensive . . .'

'You have some sore ribs,' he said curtly. 'Robbie should have landed on your hips instead — you wouldn't have felt a thing.'

'Must you always be so disgusting?'

'Just factual, my dear. You are a very well-built woman.' He stepped closer and enfolded her in his arms. 'Maida! Please, why can't we . . . ?'

'No!' Sore ribs or not she managed to writhe from his embrace with the agility of a greased eel. 'Why must you men always be thinking of the same thing? Sex!

Always sex! It makes me sick!'

'What else have you got?' Frustrated and angry Nigel glared at her, hating her all the more because she was so attractive and desirable and he wanted her to want what he wanted and she didn't. 'Brains? Money? A big car? Well, what else have you got other than what you were born with? Answer me, damn it!'

'I refuse to discuss the matter.'

'That's the trouble with you damn women!' he stormed. 'You want a man to want you but he mustn't want you because you are a female. How conceited can you get? Why the hell should any man be expected to feed you, house you, clothe and entertain you just for the sake of your company? If I just wanted something to be around I could buy a dog. If I wanted someone to wash and cook for me I'd hire a housekeeper. If I was so mad keen on intellectual conversation and simple companionship I could get that in any pub or from any friend. A man doesn't get married for those things, Maida. He gets married because he's in love and wants to cuddle the woman he's in love with. He wants good, old-fashioned sex and lots of it.'

'I think you had better go,' snapped Maida.

She stood very stiff, very straight, her lips compressed into a thin line and twin spots of colour flamed in her cheeks. She was, Nigel realized, in the very worst kind of temper. Not the shouting, screaming, hitting rages which he had experienced before and was accustomed to, but a cold, deep, acid hate which made her seem a stranger. It frightened him a little.

'Maida,' he said. 'Maida. I . . . '

'I don't want to talk about it,' she said. 'Please go.'

'I . . . ' He hesitated, not liking to leave her in such an emotional state but not knowing quite how to get her out of it without making things worse. Then his own frustration boiled over. 'Damn it,' he yelled, and aimed a vicious kick at the bed. He missed, his ankle rapping smartly against the edge of the spring and his yell echoed from the walls.

'Damn and blast the bloody thing!

Damn it all to hell!'

Painfully he limped from the room and out into the quad.

It was peaceful in the open space before the school. St Elmers was an old building and generations of rooks had nested in the tall elms their noise very reminiscent of the sound of pupils at play. Sitting on a bench beneath the trees Nigel felt himself relax and some of his anger and frustration dissolve beneath his searching self-examination.

He hadn't, he realized, been wholly fair to Maida and had offended her delicate sense of propriety by his rampant male coarseness. It was the wrong way to treat such a woman. She should be wooed with flowers and perfumes, smooth charm and constant reassurances that she was wanted for something more than the transient charm of her body. Only when so treated would she unfold the flower of her personality and offer herself, like a flower to a bee, to the more intimate delicacies of lovemaking.

And he had done a pretty good job of

crushing that flower to unrecognizable pulp.

He sighed, wishing that he had the facile charm and easy airs of, say, Ted. Ted would never have dropped such a brick.

He would have been suave and gentle, flattering and subtle, cunning as he weaved his devious path towards the desired objective. Against such a smooth worker Nigel felt somehow callow and inexperienced and he wondered if Maida felt the same. He frowned, his earlier suspicions roused by the train of thought; suspicions which had been lulled by the hectic events of the past few days. He looked up as footsteps approached, wondering if they belonged to the object of his thoughts, but it wasn't Ted who sat beside him on the bench.

Norman had, as Nigel knew he would, removed the bandage and only a smear of iodine remained where it had been. He had his pipe in his mouth and a piece of bread in his hand. He crumpled a fragment of the bread and threw it towards a cluster of sparrows eager for a free meal.

'I thought the doctor told you to take things easy for a while.'

'I am,' said Norman. He threw down more bread. 'What could be more relaxing to the mind than to sit in the sun and feed the birds?' A puff of smoke rose aromatically above his head. 'You look thoughtful,' he continued. 'Thoughtful and worried.'

'I've got reason to be worried.' Nigel dug the heel of one shoe into the ground and dragged it towards him. Critically he studied the wavering line the action had caused. 'Do you realize that we are all going to be out of work when the Head hears about last night?'

'The possibility had occurred to me,' confessed Norman. He threw down more bread. 'Want some?'

'No. What are you going to do about it?'

'Look for another job if I have to but the necessity may not arise.'

'You,' said Nigel forcefully, 'are either a supreme optimist or an unmitigated idiot. As much as the Head wants to hang onto his cheap labour he's not going to defy the vicar. Wainwright is the school padre, don't forget, and he is a man of conscience. Also he has influence in the area which we haven't and the Head would never dare to risk the school's reputation.'

'I know all about that,' said Norman calmly, 'but it doesn't change what I said.'

'Then — ?' Nigel looked hopeful for a moment then his face fell. 'No, it wouldn't work. Even if we did apologize to the vicar it wouldn't do any good. You didn't see his face last night when Ted was blowing off steam.'

'You,' said Norman patiently, 'are leaping to conclusions. I didn't say anything about continuing to work here. I said that the necessity of looking for another job may not arise.'

'Sophistry,' sneered Nigel. Norman wasn't annoyed.

'Not at all. I meant exactly what I said — or have you forgotten the luck machine?'

Nigel had forgotten, the argument with

Maida had driven the thought of it from his head but, now that Norman had reminded him the thought of what the machine could do filled him with a surge of self-confidence. Even the sun appeared to shine brighter and the song of the birds held a sweeter melody.

'The luck machine,' he breathed. 'Of course! You've no doubt that it works, Norman?'

'None, not now.' Norman threw the last of the bread towards the birds, dusted his hands, relit his pipe and settled back on the bench. 'I've been thinking about it lying up in bed,' he continued. 'It's odd how the mind refuses to accept the obvious when it is outside the common range of personal experience. And yet there is nothing unique about the luck machine at all. History is full of parallel records. All the magic swords, Excalibur, Joyeux, all the magic helmets, bracelets, belts, rings, lockets, scrolls etc., what were they but luck machines? They gave their owners or wearers special qualities. They didn't get wounded or captured or something like that. And what else was that but pure luck?'

'A combination of fortuitous circumstances,' murmured Nigel. 'It makes sense.'

'Of course it does. After all, in an infinite universe anything can, has or will happen. Anything you like to name including the discovery of the luck machine.'

'Our worries are over then,' said Nigel. He felt a little lightheaded at the extinction of his problems. Wainwright, the Head, St Elmers even, all could go cheerfully to hell while he enjoyed the fruits of endless good luck. There remained only one small fly in the ointment.

'We haven't got the machine,' he pointed out. 'Robbie still has it.'

'I know.' Norman puffed furiously at his pipe. 'I've been thinking about that too. Has anything struck you as rather odd about all this, Nigel?'

'Odd? No. What do you mean?'

'Well, Robbie's had good luck. Right?'

'Right.'

'What have the rest of us had?'

'Damn bad luck,' said Nigel promptly. He stared at his companion. 'You're getting at something,' he said slowly. 'Come on now, Norman, out with it.'

'It could all be coincidence,' mused Norman from around the stem of his pipe. 'First we had bad luck at Rolton when Robbie gave back the money he'd won. Our bad luck was that we lost all our stake money. Then you went to Wainwright and he accused you of all sorts of things and hinted that you had better start looking for another job. Bad luck there, right?'

Nigel nodded.

'Then Robbie gets a cheque for his winnings coupled with our stake money — that was his good luck. So we all went out on a celebration. Ted tried to get Robbie drunk and only managed to get whoosy himself. There was that riot and the lantern fell on the heads of those toughs. All good luck from Robbie's viewpoint. But Ted got hit on the head, Maida had her dress ruined and her ribs squashed, I got knocked out and we all got in bad with the vicar. Good luck

— bad luck. See what I mean?'

'Compensation,' said Nigel. 'Is that it?'

'I don't know and I can't be sure,' said Norman slowly. 'Obviously, for a man to be lucky things have to work to make him so. If anyone was going to be hit then it can't be him. It can be anyone else but not him. Then again, I can't get over how we missed hitting the vicar's car. The thing was right under our wheels. I don't remember much about it but, from what I do remember, it was a miracle.'

'That was the vicar's good luck, surely?'

'Perhaps, but you can never be certain of what will happen in an accident. Maybe Robbie would have been hurt had we hit — so we didn't hit.'

'It was just as well that we didn't.'

'I know but — ' Norman took the pipe from his mouth and gestured with the stem. 'Robbie was with us and so, in a manner of speaking, we were along for the ride. Robbie was the only one in the car who didn't get hurt in some way. The vicar, from what you tell me, didn't even consider the possibility of his being under the influence even though he accused the rest of us. The machine was taking care of him all the time.'

'Well it would,' said Nigel reasonably. 'That's what it's for after all. It gives him good luck.'

'Obviously — but what about the rest of us?'

'Compensation,' said Nigel again. 'It must be the answer.'

It wasn't a pleasant answer but it was the obvious one. Sitting, warm in the sunshine with the song of birds trilling from the trees, he pondered on the basic facts of the universe. It was, in a sense, a matter of give and take. Imagine a heap of ice cream of mixed flavour, vanilla and chocolate. The vanilla is good luck and the chocolate bad. Normally, anyone taking a spoonful would have some of each, perhaps a little more of one than the other but never a pure measure. Always it would be mixed. So. Assume a super spoon which could sort out the mixture so that the owner of the spoon received only vanilla ice cream — good luck. Obviously then others would have to take more than their fair share of chocolate ice cream — bad luck.

It was not a reassuring prospect for anyone who had reason to suspect that he might be the one scheduled to be given the sticky end of the exchange.

12

Alice Beecham poured water on a mound of flour, rolled up her sleeves and plunged both unwashed hands into the sticky mess. She was in the process of making a steak and kidney pudding and the heap of dough was an integral part of the recipe. A fly, unwittingly landing on the edge of the bowl, fell to its doom and was immediately incorporated into the mixture. Alice didn't notice the untimely demise or would have cared if she had. Other problems filled her mind.

The cause was her brother. Frank Winnard had a weakness which she insisted on calling that but which others tersely referred to as a vice. He liked to drink. In fact he was unable to prevent himself from yielding to temptation while there was anything to tempt him around. During term he managed, by what efforts of will only he alone could know, to restrain his tippling to the small hours but, during vacation, he tried to enjoy his holiday in the only way he knew how. Normally his sister managed to control his weakness by the simple expedient of clamping down on the purse strings but now, for some odd reason, the simple, well-tried plan refused to work.

Frank was getting liquor from somewhere and she didn't know where. It was very worrying to the simple soul and, as she dragged the mess of dough from the bowl and dumped it on a dusty board, she wondered about it. She looked up as the back door opened, half-expecting to see her wayward brother swaying on the step, but it was only the Matron and that nice Mr Bain who was staying at the school.

'Good evenin', sir. Matron.'

'Good evening,' said Ted heartily. 'Getting dinner ready?'

'I am that, sir. A nice steak and kidney pudden.'

'With onions,' said Ted. 'Lots of onions?'

'As you like, sir.'

'I do like. There's nothing like lots of

onion to give flavour to a steak and kidney pud. Right, Maida?'

'I wouldn't know,' she said stiffly. As Matron she couldn't be expected to hobnob with the lower echelons. 'I expect that Mrs Beecham knows what she is doing.'

'I expected that she does,' said Ted who had no consciousness of class distinction at all. 'Well, come on Maida, let's leave Alice to her work.'

Nigel glared at them as they entered the common room. He was slumped in a chair reading an old paper and a scrap of paper at his side bore mysterious annotations. He rose as they entered and stared at Maida.

'Where have you been?' he demanded. 'I looked everywhere for you?' He didn't add that he had looked for her to apologize for his conduct of the morning and that, as time dragged past, he had felt less and less like apologizing. Now, to see her with Ted, resurrected all his worrying suspicions.

'I went into the village,' she said coldly. 'Then I caught a bus into Rolton where I met Ted. We had lunch together. Is there anything else you would like to know?'

There was but Nigel couldn't ask. Instead he swallowed his wrath and forced himself to be casual.

'I hope that you enjoyed yourself,' he said politely. 'Did you?'

'Thank you, yes.'

'How are the ribs?'

'As well as can be expected.'

'I'm glad to hear that.' They were, thought Nigel wildly, talking more like a couple of newly-introduced strangers than as man and wife of ten years standing. 'Would you like me to get you a coffee?'

'No thank you.' She winced a little as she pressed her hand to her side. 'I think I'll have a hot bath before dinner. By the way, how is Norman?'

'Well. He had a slight headache for a while but it didn't last.'

'I see.' She moved towards the door, the Queen making a graceful exit, then halted as Ted stepped in her path.

'Now wait a minute you two,' he said. 'I don't know what the trouble is between

225

you and I don't want to know but we've more important things to do than claw each other. Now, how about kissing and becoming friends, eh?'

Neither moved.

'Come on, Nigel,' urged Ted. 'She's your wife, a beautiful woman, don't you want to kiss her?'

'Of course I do,' snapped Nigel. 'But does she want to be kissed?'

'A stupid question. You never ask any woman if she wants to be kissed. You just kiss her and see what happens.' He slapped Nigel on the shoulder. 'Well, come on, what are you waiting for?'

They kissed. For a moment it was as if Nigel had put his lips to ice and then, suddenly, she melted and returned the embrace.

'There, that's better!' Ted was beaming. 'Now, where's Norman, we've got a lot to talk about.'

'Upstairs lying down.'

'Go and get him, Nigel.'

'I'll get him,' said Maida. 'At least I'll tell him you want him.' She put a hand to her ribs again and gave a brave little smile. 'I'm really sorry but I must have that hot bath. My side, you know . . . '

This time, when she headed towards the door, no one tried to stop her.

'I've been working out some figures,' said Nigel after she'd gone. 'Now, assuming that we can start with a stake of fifty pounds and accumulate it on a five-horse selection we should make, at one meeting, about fifteen hundred pounds. That's backing the second favourite,' he explained. 'I got the odds from this old paper.'

Ted nodded, he seemed to be thinking of something else.

'Now, if we spread this around among the bookies then, in say ten meetings, we should have made . . . ' His voice died to a mumble as he recognized the other man's lack of attention. 'Something on your mind, Ted?'

'Nothing serious.' Ted made a peculiar gesture as if he were shaking himself like a dog. 'Sorry, Nigel, I was brooding on a personal problem.'

It was, Nigel hoped, not the problem he suspected. Maida's unexpected return of his kiss had woken slumbering desires about which he intended to do something at the first opportunity and he didn't want anything gumming up the works. Once the money started rolling in Maida would have nothing to worry about and neither would he. If Ted had had any ideas it was ironical that he should be the one to effectively frustrate them by his invention of the luck machine. The only advantage he'd ever had over Nigel was money and that inequality could soon be rectified.

Once they got hold of the luck machine.

'We'll get it,' promised Ted when Nigel mentioned the subject. 'Don't you worry your sweet head about that. The thing's as good as ours.'

'It is?' Norman blinked at them from the door. He had washed the iodine from his forehead but the bump rose like a one-sided horn over one eye. 'What is this, a council of war?'

'Come right in, Norman, take a chair.' Ted waved to a seat. 'We were talking about the luck machine.'

'I thought so. Did you tell Ted what we discussed, Nigel?'

'Not yet. I haven't had the chance.'

'Tell me,' urged Ted. 'I'm interested.'

Nigel told him. He made out a good case for the theory of compensation, using the analogy of the ice cream and elaborating it with a smattering of physics, organic chemistry and quantum mechanics. The additions weren't really necessary but they made the ice cream at least sound more scientific. Ted wasn't impressed.

'No,' he said firmly. 'It isn't like that at all. Luck isn't something you take from one and give to another. It is a personal thing, a selection of favourable random probabilities, and there's no compensation involved. All the things you maintained were coincidences.'

'How can you be certain?' Norman, as usual, had lit his pipe and now he blew a cloud of smoke towards the tall man. 'Look at the smoke,' he directed, as if anyone could possibly miss it. 'Call it luck. Suck some of it into a vacuum cleaner and what do you leave? An area of no-luck. Right?'

'So?'

'According to your own argument there are two kinds of luck. Positive and negative. So, if we remove the good luck then only bad luck can be left.'

'Perhaps, but we can't be sure.' Ted dismissed the demonstration with an impatient wave of his hand. 'Anyway, right or wrong, it doesn't matter. Our main concern is to get the luck machine back where it belongs. Right?'

They chorused their agreement.

'And where it belongs is with us. In the hands of cultured and intelligent people who could put it to better use than the present owner. Are we of one mind on that?'

It was a question, of course, which could only have one answer.

'Very well,' said Ted grimly. 'Now I've been very patient with Robbie about this. I've tried to act like a gentleman and politely requested the return of my own property only to be met with a blatant refusal. I then tried to be subtle and that didn't work either.' He frowned as he thought about it. 'I still can't see why he didn't get drunk,' he mused. 'That vodka was strong enough to put out a horse, let alone the pernod.'

'Never mind that,' snapped Nigel. 'It didn't work and almost got us all killed. Have you a better plan?'

'I have,' said Ted with dignity. 'All it requires is a little co-operation, swift and co-ordinated action and the ability to act for the greater good. I might also add that it cannot fail to succeed.'

'Yes?' Norman was interested. 'Tell us about it.'

'Well.' Ted coughed and then met the other's eyes. 'We have agreed that drastic measures are justifiable, haven't we?'

'No,' said Nigel. 'We didn't get that far.' He stared at Ted, a sinking feeling in his stomach. 'Let's have it,' he said patiently. 'What is this wonderful plan of yours?'

It was a simple plan, Nigel had to admit that. It depended on both a peculiarity of the human metabolism and the kinetic energy of a moving object and, he had to admit, it was hard to see how it could fail. The idea was simply to smack

Robbie on the head with a sockful of wet sand and to steal the luck machine.

'No.' Norman was emphatic. 'I'll never agree to anything like that.'

'No?' Ted searched for the scrap of paper on which Nigel had made his annotations. 'Look at this. Nigel worked it out. With an initial stake of fifty pounds — I can sell the car for more than that — we could clear, in ten meetings about a million apiece.' He squinted at the scribbled figures. 'It is a million, isn't it, Nigel?'

'About that.'

'Well then, call it a round million. A million pounds each! Think of it, Norman!'

'I am thinking of it.'

'Keep it in mind,' urged Ted. 'Now it isn't as if we were going to hurt Robbie in any way. I've done some reading on the matter and a sockful of wet sand is relatively harmless. It will leave a light contusion and perhaps a mild headache but that is all. In fact it will be no worse than what you suffered yourself when you hit your head on the windscreen. That didn't kill you, did it?'

'No,' admitted Norman slowly, 'it didn't kill me but that's beside the point. Who wants to spend the next five years in jail?'

'No one, and no one's going to jail at all. Robbie will never know what has hit him. It will be all over in a flash.'

'I don't like it,' protested Nigel. 'Trying to get him drunk was one thing, smacking him over the head and robbing him is another.'

'Where's the difference?' Ted, eyes flashing behind his spectacles, hair in wild disarray from the impatient thrust of his fingers, marched up and down the common room as he pressed home his argument. 'Anyway, how can it be robbery? We gave him the machine to test, didn't we? We allowed him to participate in a scientific experiment — and look at what it cost us? Robbie's got twelve hundred pounds of our money, don't forget. Twelve hundred!'

It was a telling argument. There were others, all of equal weight and all adding up to the same thing. With the luck machine they would be laughing; without it they were lost. It was, as Ted kept pointing out, a simple matter of self-preservation.

The rest was merely a matter of detail.

13

Zero hour was at eleven that night. As the clock chimed in the old tower three muffled shapes left the school and wended down the road towards the pond at Willard's Copse. Ted, with a flash of sheer genius unequalled by Machiavelli at his best, had telephoned Robbie's friend, pretended that he was an official of the BBC, and had asked for a night recording of wild pond life to be taken at one o'clock precisely. The recording, he'd explained, was to be used in a cultural exchange with the Soviet Union and hinted that both recognition and reward would attend successful results.

There was no doubt that Robbie would be called in to assist thus placing the victim at the right place at the right time.

Nigel had protested.

'What about Robbie's friend?'

'What about him?' Ted had been casual. 'Push him in the mud and, if he gets obstreperous, bang him over the head. He won't cause trouble. Now, are you sure that you can get the stockings?'

Nigel had obtained the stockings though, what Maida would say when she discovered three pairs of her precious nylons had mysteriously vanished he hated to think. But he would make it up to her, he promised himself, more than make it up. Idly he wondered if it were possible to buy pure gold stockings. Probably not and they would be too heavy if he could. Well, he would settle for a stocking factory and a diamond-studded suspender belt. She should appreciate that.

He grunted as he bumped into something before him. The night was pitch dark without a hint of moon behind the heavy clouds and only a familiar scent told him that the object before him was Norman. Ted stood to one side, a deeper shadow in the darkness.

'You'd better kill that pipe, Norman,' he rapped. 'You can smell that stuff you smoke a mile away. The stockings, Nigel?'

'Here.' Nigel barely restrained himself

from adding a respectful 'sir' as he handed them over. Ted had obviously entered into the spirit of the thing and was imagining himself to be an intrepid commander of a gallant patrol deep in enemy territory where the slightest mistake could mean discovery and death. The trouble was that his enthusiasm was catching.

'Keep one pair for yourself,' commanded the leader. 'There's some loose dirt here so load one with it like this.'

He stopped in the darkness, apparently imagining that his companions had infra-red vision or were equipped with X-ray eyes. Scuffling sounds came as he clawed at the dirt. He hefted his stocking, grunted, added more dirt and was satisfied.

'Here.' He passed it to Nigel. 'I'd better do it. Unless we get the weight just right we may as well hit him with a feather.'

The stocking he passed Nigel was no feather. He hefted it, trying to imagine what it would feel like swung against his own skull and shuddered.

'It's pretty heavy, Ted.'

'It has to be. You don't want to take a long swing, remember. Just hold it in your hand and bring it down.' He passed the weapon to Norman. 'Here, you take this while I fill my own.'

Fully armed the little band continued on its way. Ahead of them the pond at Willard's Copse signalled its presence by a strong odour of rotting weed, slimy mud, stagnant water and the unmistakable scent of animal droppings. The local farmer, Nigel remembered, watered his cows at the pond as well as his horses. A discordant melody of frogs rent the night air with a cacophony of sound. Silence fell as they neared the undergrowth around the area.

'Notice that?' Ted was more than ever the skilled commander conscious of the slightest danger. 'Listen, can you hear it?'

'Hear what?' Nigel strained his ears.

'Can you, Norman?'

'I can't hear a thing,' snapped Norman. Without the comfort of his pipe he had little time for games.

'Exactly. You can't hear a thing. The frogs aren't croaking and they should be croaking. Robbie would know that and be warned. We must get into position and remain still so that they start croaking again.'

'For two hours?' Norman was horrified.

'No. Robbie knows the habits of these creatures as well as I do. He is to take the recording at one o'clock precisely and my bet is that he'll be here a full hour before then. Now, stockings on for disguise!'

Dutifully they rolled the second stocking of each pair over their heads.

'I can't see,' yelped Nigel.

'I can't breathe,' said Norman in a muffled voice. His voice became clearer as he lifted the obstruction. 'Damn it, Ted, do we have to wear these?'

'Do you want to be recognized?' Ted, apparently thought that Robbie and his friend had infra-red vision too, but he was willing to compromise. 'Leave them rolled up just over the eyebrows,' he ordered. 'When the time comes to attack roll them down.'

'How are we going to see who to attack?' asked Nigel sarcastically. 'Personally I can't see a single thing.'

'If you can't see then they can't either,' pointed out Ted. 'But here, take this, you too Norman.' He thrust a small flashlight into each hand. 'I bought them in Rolton,' he explained. 'I guessed we'd find a use for them.'

It was just another facet of his cool, calculating, military type mind or, as Nigel thought, a true measure of his crafty, cunning anticipation. Thrusting the flashlight into his pocket, swinging the loaded stocking with his right hand, he pressed into the undergrowth surrounding the pond.

It smelt. It smelt and it was damp and crawling things had an unhealthy interest in his face, neck and hands. He wished that he could smoke or, alternatively, he wished that he had never come. Nigel thought longingly of Maida and the warm, soft bed in which she lay at this very moment. He would have been better off expending his energy trying to persuade her to let him share that bed instead of crouching out here in the night among a lot of cow and horse dung by the side of a stinking pond.

If this was adventure, he thought bitterly, then those who liked it could have it. Personally he would take his in future via the printed page.

Footsteps sounded down the road and the frogs, who had been making the night hideous with their croaking, suddenly fell silent.

'It's them!' Nigel almost leapt from his skin as a figure rose at his side and a strained voice whispered in his ear. Ted, like any good commander, was making the rounds. 'Listen! They're coming!'

'Hooray for them,' snarled Nigel in a whisper. 'What do we do now, cheer?'

'Stocking down,' rapped Ted. 'Weapon ready. No talking and when you strike strike hard.'

He vanished into the night, only a muffled curse as he slipped on something betraying his presence. A startled yelp from halfway around the pond showed that Norman too had been surprised by the unexpected appearance of his leader. Silence fell again as the footsteps came closer.

Robbie was in the lead. Nigel, his eyes

now accustomed to the darkness, could recognize his silhouette against the lighter shadows of the sky. His footsteps too were unmistakable, their sound altering as he stepped from the road towards the pond. Behind him a smaller figure scampered in his wake.

'You know, my dear Wilding,' he said excitedly, 'we really must get an excellent recording tonight. Think of it! An actual exchange with the Soviet Union! One hardly dares to imagine to what this could lead!'

'I am glad that you called me, Charles,' said Robbie's mechanical voice from the darkness. 'I think that we shall get all we came for. I must say that I have been very fortunate in such things lately.'

I'll bet you have, thought Nigel as he crouched in the undergrowth. With our machine strapped to your fat wrist you couldn't be anything else. And what are you doing with it? Helping your friends and colleagues? Not on your life! Bird watching, that's what. Bird watching and me practically out of a job and on the relief!

The unfairness of it all firmed his resolution. The little man needn't be harmed, one push would settle his hash, but Robbie was something else. He was big, strong and would put up a fight if given half a chance. Well, he wasn't going to be given half a chance. One hit and that would be that.

He leaned forward, craning his neck and straining his eyes. A flash of light showed a momentary glimpse of the two figures as they stooped over the tape recorder. Neither man spoke, old hands at the game they knew the value of silence, and even the flash of light was not repeated. Nigel sucked in his breath and rolled down the stocking over his eyes. The fabric cut down his vision even more so he groped forward like a blind man. Fuming he pulled the material away from his face and poked holes in it with a fingernail. Restoring his disguise he moved forward to the attack.

Something squashed beneath his foot.

He cursed under his breath, moved cautiously away from the redolent mass and dropped to his hands and knees.

Something squashed under his left hand.

He swore again and rose to his feet, wiping his hand on the loaded stocking to clean it from the mess. Suddenly impatient he strode to where he imagined the couple to be, forgetting in his excitement the flashlight in his jacket pocket.

Something touched his left shoulder.

He yelled, nerves snapping beneath the strain and swung wildly at what stood behind him. The loaded stocking crashed through the undergrowth, hit something solid and burst with a shower of damp soil. He grunted as something lashed him across the face, tearing the disguise from his head, and scratching his cheeks. Desperately he fought to free himself from the monster which had engulfed him, tearing free of the branches just as a light flashed to one side.

Stars burst in his head and then he was falling to end with a splash in the stagnant pond. Dimly, above the sound of the water, he heard a shout, the sound of running feet and a shriek as if someone had stepped into a bear-trap. Then he went under with weeds wrapping themselves lovingly around him as if determined never to let him go. Clawing, spitting water, tearing at the weeds he surfaced and waded to the side of the pond, cursing Ted, his brilliant idea, the luck machine and everything else he could think of. Soggily he crawled to firmer ground, rose to his feet, headed towards the road and then tripped over something soft which moaned as he fell.

Lights shone from somewhere down the road.

A thing lay revealed in the reflected glow. It had a peculiar copper-coloured skin, great bulges where the eyes should have been and a long, limp appendage hanging from the top of its head. Nigel grabbed it, pulled it free and stared into Ted's bleary eyes.

'Ted!'

'Quick,' gasped Ted. 'Let's get out of here!'

He was still the leader and still to be obeyed especially when he had ordered a strategic retreat. Like any good leader he set an example, fading into the night as if coated with invisible paint, and Nigel did his best to follow. He was foiled by two things. One was the sodden state of his clothing which made fast motion impossible. The other was the tape recorder which was lying close by.

He kicked it, tripped, and went hurtling through the air to land with a wet squelch at the edge of the pond. Gravity did the rest. For the second time he felt the foetid waters close above his head. When he rose to the surface he had company.

The lights had belonged to a police car making a random patrol and it had halted by the side of the copse. A uniformed sergeant, huge in silhouette with the headlights behind him, stood at the edge of the pond, careful not to step into the mud. He called anxiously to Nigel as he spat out a mouthful of water.

'Are you all right, sir?'

Nigel was far from being all right but, by the time he had reached the shore, he had decided to go down with colours flying. A strong hand gripped his wrist and hauled him from danger. A flashlight glared into his face and he squinted against the light.

'Do you have to do that?'

'Just routine, sir,' said the man, but the light moved away. 'Been having a little trouble here, sir?'

'Not exactly, officer.'

'Sergeant Kent's the name, sir. Sergeant Gordon Kent. And yours?'

Nigel told him, wondering why the man was so polite and yet glad that he was. Then he lost the feeling of gladness, remembering the new, psychological approach favoured by some members of the constabulary. It was a technique which had been perfected in interrogation and consisted of first making the victim feel that he had met a friend and then proving to him that the old adage that you can't trust a soul still had teeth.

'Now, sir,' said the sergeant casually. 'Would you like to tell me what all this is about?'

'I . . . ' Nigel swallowed. 'I was going for a walk,' he said desperately. 'I thought I heard someone cry out in here, a cry of pain, so I came to see if I could render assistance.' He managed to give a shaky laugh. 'I must have tripped over something and landed in the pond.'

'Is that all, sir?' The light moved back into his face. 'Are you sure that is all?'

'Well . . . ' Nigel hesitated, not knowing whether it was wise to say too much or too little. 'I seem to remember that there was someone here after all. At least I gained that impression.'

'Over here, sergeant,' called another uniformed man. His light shone on a stocking hanging grotesquely from a branch. 'And here's another.' His light picked out the one Nigel had pulled from Ted's head. 'Two of them at least.'

'What's this?' The sergeant stared down at the tape-recorder illuminated by his flashlight. 'Is this yours, sir?'

'No,' said Nigel, wondering desperately where the owners were. Probably beaten into insensibility somewhere and he felt a cold sweat at what would happen to him if they were found in that unhappy state. He yelped as a tall, familiar figure suddenly loomed in the glow of the headlights.

'What? What's happening here?' Charles scampered from behind the shield of Robbie's body and stared at the assembled policemen. 'What's all this about?'

'Robbie!' Nigel appealed to his colleague. 'Are you all right?'

'Is that you, Lloyd?' Robbie jerked forward and peered into his face. 'Why, my dear fellow, what are you doing here?'

It was a question which couldn't truthfully be answered: you can hardly tell a man who is looming over you that you intended to knock him senseless and steal his property, but the police had questions of their own and Nigel willingly yielded priority. Gradually the whole business began to make some sort of official sense.

'I see,' mused the sergeant thoughtfully. 'So you two gentlemen came here, set up your tape recorder and then moved some distance down the road. Is that correct?'

'Perfectly correct, sergeant,' babbled the little man. 'The recorder can be pre-set to begin operating at a selected time. That avoids the need for an operator to be in constant attendance. It is,' he added modestly, 'a slight improvement of my own and the details are to be published in *Wild Life*, the issue after next.'

'And then, sir?'

'Well, we set it and moved away. Wild life is extremely sensitive to the presence of humans, sergeant, you will note that the frogs, for example, are not making their normal sounds at present, that is because we have disturbed them. It was essential that we . . . '

Nigel, leaning against a prickly shrub, felt a little as Napoleon must have felt when he realized that the Moscow campaign was a bust. Ted had overlooked the obvious and the results had been inevitable. The victim had been safely away when they had moved in to the attack and, blinded with the stocking disguise, overtense with nervous strain, they had hit out at anything which moved.

And the only thing moving in the copse had been themselves.

'Well,' said the sergeant, 'it seems pretty obvious what must have happened. Do you often walk this way, sir?'

'Uh?' Nigel straightened as he realized that he was expected to answer. 'Well, not all that often, but I like a constitutional before turning in. It clears the brain,' he added wildly. 'Blows away the scholastic fug.'

'Do any of the other masters?'

'I don't know. Some of them, I expect. Why?'

'This was a trap,' said Kent solemnly. 'A gang of young hooligans must have thought it a bright idea to lurk in the copse and spring out at any passersby. It's my guess they would have stolen the recorder if you hadn't interfered. You were very fortunate, sir.'

'Was I?' Nigel didn't think so.

'They must have lost their nerve,' said the sergeant. 'The vicious swine had a stocking loaded with dirt and, if I know anything about the type, they would have cracked your skull without a second thought. It's lucky we came along when we did.'

'Yes,' said Nigel. 'Yes, I suppose that it was.'

'It was,' emphasized the sergeant. 'A lot

of people sneer at the police but if it wasn't for us this country wouldn't be worth living in.' He was obviously a man who didn't believe in wasting an opportunity to drive home an important lesson.

Nigel made dutiful noises of appreciation.

'You should get straight home, sir,' said the sergeant generously. He gestured towards the police car. 'You'd better . . . ' he stared at Nigel's condition and hastily changed his mind, ' . . . run all the way,' he said firmly. 'The exertion will do you good.'

14

'A fiasco!' Ted slammed his hand on the common room table. 'A first-class fiasco! It's a pity,' he sneered, 'that I couldn't have had with me two men of initiative and enterprise. Wellington said that, given two such men, he could have ruled the world.'

'Napoleon,' corrected Norman from behind his pipe. 'It was Napoleon who said that.'

'Well, whoever it was he was right,' snapped Ted. 'I've never met such a couple of stumble-bums in my life! A fiasco, that's what it was.'

'A betrayal, you mean!' Nigel, bathed, changed but still smarting from his wounds, added more liquid from the bottle of scotch Ted had donated to the discussion and stirred his coffee. 'A stinking, lousy betrayal!'

'A strategic retreat,' corrected Ted. 'Any good commander knows when it is time to leave the field of action.'

'Leaving his men behind?' Nigel sipped at the coffee. 'And you, Norman? What happened to you?'

Norman, it appeared, had been winded during the fracas and had crouched, gasping for breath as the police arrived. Nigel's splashing as he crawled from his second trip into the pond had provided sufficient distraction for him to leave the area unnoticed. It was, he pointed out, the beneficent workings of fate.

'All right,' said Nigel crossly. 'But who hit me? That's what I want to know.'

'That must have been me,' confessed Ted. He lifted a hand before Nigel could give tongue to what was on his mind. 'You can't blame me! I told you all to wear your disguises. I caught a glimpse of a naked head, thought that it belonged to Robbie and let fly. I realized my mistake almost at once.'

'And then?'

'Then Norman and I met in the dark. We swung together.' Ted winced as he rubbed the side of his neck. 'He almost killed me.'

'I wish that he had,' snapped Nigel viciously. He drained his cup of coffee and refilled it from the pot, slopping in more liquid from the bottle. 'I supposed you winded Norman in return?'

'He did.' Norman was grim. 'Remind me to show him what a stocking half full of dirt can do when swung against the human solar plexus.'

'I can imagine,' said Ted hastily. He scowled darkly down at the table. 'A failure,' he summarized. 'No matter how you look at it the attempt was a failure.'

'Naturally.' Norman helped himself to the communal bottle. 'What else did you expect? We warned you that the law of compensation would come into effect. Now, perhaps, you'll believe us.'

'Uh!'

'It's true. Every time Robbie gets good luck we get bad.'

'All right, all right, you don't have to keep on about it!' Ted, Nigel could see, was a rattled man. He scowled down at the table as if coming to a momentous decision. 'We've been too gentle,' he announced. 'Even tonight we were afraid of hurting him, well, that weakening line of thought has to stop. Empires were not built by cowards! Kingdoms are not won by the faint-hearted! We must strike and strike hard and strike to win!'

'Hear, hear!' applauded Nigel. 'What are you talking about?'

'We have a fortune within our grasp,' continued Ted. 'Are we going to sit back and let it slip away? No! A thousand times no!'

'I think,' said Norman drily, 'that we can dispense with the propaganda. What's on your mind?'

'Winnard has a shotgun. I suggest that one of us use it.'

'You're mad!'

'No, Nigel, not mad. I'm a realist.' Ted looked at their faces. 'Oh, I'm not suggesting that we kill him. All we have to do is to fire a round over his head and demand the return of the luck machine. It's as simple as that.'

'And when he goes to the police?'

'He won't go. What can he say if he does? They will laugh at the very idea of a luck machine and probably think that he's touched in the head. They won't,' added Ted darkly, 'be so very far wrong at that. But you're all forgetting something. We'll have the luck machine and it will work as well for us as it does for Robbie.'

'Exactly.' Norman looked sagely at his companions through a cloud of smoke. 'Haven't either of you grasped the full implications of the thing? If you tried to use a shotgun on Robbie it would probably blow your head off. Can't you realize that the luck machine is defending its owner?'

'Of course,' snapped Nigel, 'but — '

'There are no 'buts' about it. What makes Robbie lucky? The machine. What could be the worse sort of luck to befall him? Losing the machine, of course. Therefore, by common logic, the machine will work to safeguard Robbie's possession of it. If it works at all, and we know that it does work, then the harder we try to get it from him the greater the odds are stacked against us.'

Nigel whistled with dismay. 'I never thought of that.'

'Well, think of it now.'

'Cunning,' said Ted. 'Very cunning but, damn it, very true.' He rose and paced the floor, gnawing his lower lip with irritation. 'You're right, Norman,' he finally decided. 'It's like one of those old tales from the Arabian Nights. You know, the thing about the magic bottle or whatever it was. You can give it away or sell it but you can't be robbed of it. It has to be disposed of by an act of volition.' He ground the fist of one hand into the palm of the other. 'Damn it! We were fools! We should never have left it so late!'

They were curious.

'The thing is increasing its potential. I worked out some problematical figures on expected performance and, as I suspected, it's in a geometrical ratio. At first we may have been able to get it away from him, by force if we had to, but not now. Norman's right in what he says. It's a kind of reverse action and any harmful influence aimed at Robbie will recoil on the instigator's own head.' He became very thoughtful. 'Norman! Nigel! I take it that neither of you is a coward?'

'Well,' said Nigel cautiously. 'I don't

know about that.'

'Have some more scotch. Norman?'

'I do know. I'm a coward.'

'No you're not, not really. You are just being modest. Here, have another drink.' Ted sloshed liquid from the bottle into their cups of coffee. 'I don't want to harp on this because men of your intelligence and discernment will have grasped the terrible danger inherent in Robbie and the luck machine. You will also have realized the necessity for stopping him before it is too late. As yet he hasn't realized his own potential but, when he does — !' He gestured with the half-full bottle in his hand. 'Gentlemen! He must be stopped!'

'You said that he couldn't be stopped,' pointed out Nigel.

'I know. I was too hasty. There is a way.'

'How?' Norman was practical.

'By sacrifice! By a man of keen intellect and staunch moral fibre recognizing the terrible danger and who is determined to stop it. By a hero. By a man who is willing to be a martyr.' Ted lowered the bottle and looked at each in turn. 'I am not the man,' he said with becoming modesty. 'I admit my own limitations. But you, Nigel, you are of a different calibre.'

'Uh?'

'Drink up, old man and have some more.' Again Ted tilted the bottle. 'Listen,' he said. 'Robbie is in his room now fast asleep. You creep in and, without a second thought, brain him with this bottle. I'll take care of the rest.'

'I bet you will.' Nigel frowned at his coffee wondering why all the scotch Ted had poured into it hadn't affected him in the slightest degree. 'Didn't we just decide that if anyone tried any rough stuff with our friend he would get it back double?'

'We did,' said Ted calmly. 'That is why I am asking for volunteers. You will try, Nigel, and you may succeed. If you do then, no matter what happens to you, a place will be reserved for you in the halls of fame. If you fail then Norman will . . .'

'Norman will do nothing of the kind,' he snapped. 'Think of something else!'

'We could hypnotize him,' suggested Nigel. 'We could make him think that the luck machine is red hot, or something and that he has to get rid of it. Or we . . . '

'Oh, shut up!' Ted was disgusted with the pair of them and showed it. He sipped his coffee, scowled, added more fluid from his bottle, sipped and scowled again. 'What the devil?' He tilted the bottle to his lips and spat a spray across the room. 'Tea!' he howled. 'Cold tea! I've been robbed!'

Lunging to his feet he darted from the room and returned carrying a second, unopened bottle. Carefully he examined the sealed cap, grunted, opened it and took a sip of the contents.

'Tea!' he slammed the bottle down on the table so hard that Nigel thought it would break. 'Someone's switched the scotch for cold tea!'

'Maybe the place where you bought it?' suggested Nigel. Ted waved him to silence.

'Winnard!' he said after a moment's thought. 'I caught him prowling about my room and believed him when he said that he was polishing the floor. Why, the dirty, low-down scoundrel! I'll kill him for this!'

'He's a big man,' warned Nigel.

'Never mind that! I'll . . . ' Ted broke off, a sudden, happy smile illuminating his features. 'No I won't,' he decided. 'For several reasons in fact. He is, as you say, a big man and I cannot envisage myself brawling with one of the lower orders; I cannot prove anything anyway but, most of all, he has given me an idea. He was subtle, do you understand? Subtle.'

'So?'

'He used his brains — what he has of them. He didn't just steal the liquor, he exchanged it. Well, we can play the same game.' He smiled at their blank expressions. 'Without me,' he said grandly, 'where would you be? It takes a little something extra for a man to be able to recognize an opportunity and act on it. Fleming was such a man. Edison, Benjamin Franklin, Rothschild, all men of genius.' His mood changed as he met their bewildered stares. 'For crying out loud,' he stormed, 'can't you see it even yet? We make a second luck machine, or rather something that looks exactly like the one Robbie is wearing. Then, when the right time comes, we switch one for the other. He'll never know.'

'He may not,' pointed out Norman. 'But what about the machine itself? Will it let him be so unlucky as to accept a substitute?'

'That,' said Ted with an evil leer, 'depends on just how it is done.' Absent-mindedly he picked up the bottle as if to pour a toast, remembered what it contained and snorted his disgust. 'Hell,' he said. 'Let's all go to bed.'

They were busy after that. They were busy all the next morning and for the next few days. Ted, surprisingly, seemed to be in no great hurry. He fussed over the substitute luck machine, altering this and changing that and generally acting like a man with something on his mind. He vanished for long periods of time, driving off in his car, usually with Maida and mostly with both her and Robbie. Then, unaccountably, he remained at the school while Robbie, as usual, went on his own, mysterious errands. Maida, to Nigel's astonishment, accompanied him.

Ted was casual when he mentioned it.

'You can't expect a woman like Maida to hang around this crummy place during her holiday,' he said. 'In fact I suggested that she go around with Robbie a little and she agreed with me that it would be a kind and humane thing to do.'

'She wanted to accompany him?' Nigel was shaken. 'She wanted to accompany Robbie? *Robbie?*'

'You underestimate the man,' said Ted airily. 'He knows an awful lot about all sorts of things. Brass rubbings, medieval domestic implements, stamps, birds, the early days of the cinema . . . all sorts of interesting things.'

'Someone,' said Nigel savagely, 'is taking someone else for all kinds of a fool.'

'Maida is no fool,' said Ted. He leaned back on the bench on which they were both sitting and stared idly at the tops of the elms across the quad. 'Neither is Robbie, inhuman though he might appear to be. Has it ever occurred to you that he might be a very lonely man?'

'What has that got to do with it?'

'A great deal. Take a lonely man, add a

beautiful and attractive woman, what do you get?'

'Trouble!' Nigel reared up as though stung. 'Lots of trouble — from me!'

'Calm down,' said Ted evenly. 'Everything is under control. All Maida is doing is to make Robbie feel relaxed so that he will act a little more like a normal human being and less like a mechanized monk. It is, if you like, an act of charity. We are, in a sense, casting our bread upon the waters . . .'

'So that we get it back soaking wet?'

'So that we get it back a thousand fold,' said Ted, ignoring the interruption. 'The trouble with you, Nigel, is that you have a limited imagination. You seem unable to grasp the big picture. Here you are, squawking about property rights as if you were a case-hardened Victorian who regarded his wife as a personal possession. Maida is an individual in her own right, not a slave or a chattel. If she wants to go out for a walk with Robbie how can you stop her?'

He couldn't and Nigel knew it. Maida was strong-willed at the best of times and now, when their personal relationship left much to be desired, she would defy him for the sheer pleasure of asserting her independence. Irritably he chewed at his lower lip.

'What's on your mind, Ted?'

'I beg your pardon?'

'You heard what I said. What mad idea are you working on now?'

'Well — '

'Is Maida a part of it? Is she?'

'Well,' admitted Ted, 'yes, she is. I was going to tell you about it,' he said hastily as he saw Nigel's expression. 'There's no need to get all upset. There's nothing underhand going on. It was just that . . . well, that . . . '

'Go on,' said Nigel grimly.

'Well, you are inclined to be a bit hasty and I wasn't sure . . . '

'That I would agree to you using my wife to further your schemes? You're damn right I wouldn't.'

'Our schemes, Nigel,' reminded Ted stiffly. 'We are all in this together, don't forget. You, me, Norman, Maida . . . '

'Her too? Since when?'

'Since she forced the details out of me.' Ted looked embarrassed. 'She guessed more than we thought. Those stockings, for example, she missed them and, well, I had to tell her the truth. She was most upset.'

'I bet she was,' Nigel agreed. 'Three pairs of nylons mean a lot to Maida.'

'She was so upset that she felt she should report the matter to the police. I finally managed to persuade her that it would be an unwise thing to do and finally she agreed with me. That was after I had told her all about the luck machine.'

'Brilliant!' Nigel cast his eyes towards Heaven. 'Really brilliant!'

'I covered up,' insisted Ted. 'I warned her of the danger of the thing, you know, the potential flash-back reaction.'

'Naturally.' Nigel lowered his eyes and aimed them at his companion. 'Just when,' he said coldly, 'did you have this cosy little chat with my wife?'

'When . . . ' Ted eased his collar. 'When I asked her to help us substitute the machine.'

'And how did you propose she should do that?'

It was typical of all Ted's harebrained schemes. It was simply that Maida should so entice Robbie that he would be a gone goose and amiable to any suggestion. The suggestion, of course, would be that he remove the luck machine and hand it to her for some reason. She would then hand back the substitute and the thing would be done. On the subject of just when all this was to take place and in what circumstances Ted was maddeningly vague.

'How do you know that Robbie will fall for her line?' Nigel, unable to sit, had risen and was tramping up and down before the bench like an hysterical sentry. 'Why couldn't we have done it ourselves? Gone swimming or something? Robbie hates women anyway.'

'Wrong!' Ted held up his hand, fingers outstretched. 'He doesn't smoke, drink, gamble, or beat harmless animals. So what's left? Women, that's what.'

'You're joking. Robbie's never looked at a girl.'

'No? What about that dancer at the Purple Dragon? Do you think that her clothes fell off by accident? They fell off because Robbie's subconscious desires were at work and for no other reason. The same with the buxom faggot at the next table. The drinks we slipped him repressed his censor just sufficient to let his true self through. I'll bet that, had we waited, every wench in the place would have wound up as bare as an egg. Girls are his weak spot, Nigel old boy, and I guessed it. We've found his Achilles Heel and set a Delilah to crop his whiskers. The trap has been set and all we've got to do is to wait for the jaws to snap close. The luck machine is as good as ours!'

'But — '

'But what?' Ted, riding the crest of his own enthusiasm, was impossible to stop. 'What are you worrying about? Maida's a shrewd woman and able to take care of herself. She knows what to do and how to do it. Once she switches on her charm Robbie will just roll over and stick his legs in the air. I tell you, Nigel, we can't lose!'

His enthusiasm was contagious. Nigel,

quelling his instinctive doubts, warmed to the thoughts of riches to come. A million? Bah! Ten million, a hundred, there would be no stopping them once they had got started, the wealth of the world would be theirs!

'We'll look after Robbie,' said Nigel generously.

'Of course we'll look after him.' Ted was expansive. 'We'll give him the few odd thousand as a consolation prize.' He leaned back stretching his arms and inflating his chest. 'Doesn't it feel wonderful to be rich?'

'More than wonderful,' agreed Nigel devoutly. With the luck machine as good as delivered he felt enchanted.

The feeling lasted until late that evening.

15

Maida didn't come home. That was bad enough but Robbie failed to return also and, to Nigel's fevered imagination, there was only one reason for their absence. Ted tried to calm him down.

'They could be seeing a late film or having a late meal,' he pointed out. 'It's early yet.'

'It's almost midnight. The last bus has left Stark and it's a long walk from Rolton.'

'They could be visiting some of Robbie's friends,' suggested Norman. He had been briefed on the latest scheme but had said nothing, engrossing himself with his pipe as the others made grandiose plans. 'He knows a lot of people in the area.'

'That must be it,' Ted agreed. 'There's a hundred reasons why they aren't back yet. Robbie's an odd one, he may have decided to walk home, or listen to a rare bird or something. Stop worrying, Nigel, everything will be all right.'

Nigel hoped so. His warm enthusiasm of the afternoon had vanished to be replaced by a mounting trepidation. Desperately he tried to remember one of Ted's ideas which had worked as hoped and came up with a dull and aching zero. Nothing the tall man had instigated had ever followed an expected path. Trouble had followed him like the footprints of a drunk in the snow. Trouble had attended every moment of his stay at St Elmers. Trouble, thought Nigel grimly, and Ted seemed to be identical twins. Trouble, that is, for someone else.

Irritably he crossed the creaking floor of the common room and stared into the night. Below the window the quad shone in the faint starlight, the gravel of the drive a lighter shadow against the rest, the twin pillars of the gates ghostly sentinels in the darkness. An owl hooted from one of the ancient elms.

From the tower the clock struck midnight.

From behind him came the riffle of a pack of cards.

'How about a little poker to pass the time?' Ted fanned the deck again. 'Straight draw, no wild deuces, aces high and three card maximum draw.'

'With only the three of us?' Nigel didn't turn from his vigil.

'Any pair openers,' urged Ted. 'Come on, Nigel, you can't stand there all night.'

'I'm not going to stand here all night,' snapped the distraught husband. 'I'm giving them one more hour and then I notify the police. They could have had an accident or something. I . . . ' He broke off, craning forward and cursing as his forehead bumped the glass. 'Damn!'

'See anything?' Norman had moved quietly to his side.

'A flash of light, it could have been the headlights of a car. See? There it goes again.' His heart gave a sudden bound of relief as a car turned through the gates. 'It's them!'

'Sit down,' snapped Ted, the general rapping orders to his men. 'Don't let them see you. Take a hand and pretend to be playing, we don't want Robbie to get suspicious.'

He was talking good sense. If Maida had thought to annoy him by deliberately staying out so late then Nigel was just the man to show her how little he cared. Lighting a cigarette he squinted at the cards Ted flung towards him. Four kings, not bad at all, a pity that it wasn't a real hand in a real game. Hopefully he tried to rectify the error.

'Open for five,' he said carelessly. 'Five shillings, that is. Norman?'

Maida entered the room before he could answer. She looked flushed, excited and her eyes held a dangerous sparkle. Her lipstick, Nigel noted sourly, was smudged.

'Where's Robbie?' Ted, as ever, paid no attention to details.

'He went straight to his room.' She laughed, a gay, light-hearted tinkle of merriment. The heroines of the romantic novels she had enjoyed when a girl had laughed like that. Nigel thought she was drunk.

'Did you get it?' Ted was impatient. 'Maida, for Pete's sake! I can't stand the strain. Did you get it?'

'Well . . . ' She deliberately paused, enjoying her moment to the full. Nigel, failing to catch her eye, exploded in sudden wrath.

'Where the hell have you been?' he stormed. 'Necking in a hedge?'

'I beg your pardon?'

'Don't give me that stuff!' Anxiety had been replaced by rage and all his pre-determined casualness had vanished like a puff of smoke. He had intended to sit at the table, a cigarette in his mouth, the cards in his hand and, perhaps, to raise an eyebrow in casual greeting. That, if nothing else, would have shown her just how much he was master of the situation. That would have shown her how invulnerable he was to the sordid pangs of jealousy. So much for good intentions.

'Look at the time!' he yelled. 'Almost one in the morning! I want to know where you've been.'

'I've been out,' she said coldly. 'With a gentleman.'

'Some gentleman,' he sneered. 'What happened to your lipstick?'

'Nothing.'

'Nothing? It's smeared half over your face and you stand there and tell me that! Me! Your husband!'

'Please!' She stared from one to the other, her eyes shining and her teeth biting at her bottom lip. 'I feel rather tired. I think that I'd better go straight to bed. My ribs . . . ' Gently she pressed a hand to her side, ' . . . I don't really feel strong enough for a public argument. Goodnight, all.'

'Wait!' yelled Ted.

'Yes, wait!' echoed Nigel furiously. He was damned if she was going to rob him of the pleasure of a quarrel. 'Now you listen to me!'

'Nigel, for Heaven's sake shut up!' Ted glared his anger and appealed to Norman. 'Can't you keep this maniac quiet?'

'It's his wife,' said Norman dubiously.

'It's our future.'

'You're right.' Norman grabbed Nigel by the arm and jerked him to one side. 'Shut up!' he ordered. 'If you want to quarrel do it somewhere else. Personally I find all this nonsense very embarrassing.'

'Sorry,' said Nigel, deflating as suddenly

as he had inflated. He had, he realized, made himself look rather a fool. Worse, he had put his foot in it again with Maida and, as he knew, the thing she detested most was a public scene. Humbly he watched the expert swing into action.

'There, there,' soothed Ted as he led Maida to a chair. 'You've had a hard time and I know it if others don't. Now just sit down and rest yourself for a while. Would you like some coffee?'

'No thank you.'

'It will only take a moment. Nigel, would you get Maida a nice hot cup of coffee please?'

'No really, I couldn't touch another drop. We had to wait for a taxi to be free so we sat and talked in a coffee bar until it called for us. You know,' she said dreamily, 'Eric is a very unusual man.'

'That he is,' said Ted heartily. 'Did you manage . . . ?'

'He knows the most fascinating things,' she continued, ignoring Ted's crude attempts to get to the heart of things. 'I could have sat and listened to him for hours and hours. He's travelled too, almost all over the world. Do you know that he once hitch-hiked to Turkey and back?'

'No, but . . . '

'He went all on his own. Just took a haversack and set off. There aren't many men with that kind of courage nowadays.' The look she flung at Nigel left no doubt as to whom she had in mind. 'And he's got ambition. He's studied politics and economics and all sorts of things like that. He's got a degree in ancient history and he knows several languages. He's kind and gentle and considerate and he has the highest respect for women. Do you know,' she smiled with pleasant reminiscence, 'that he didn't even try to kiss me? Not once! If that doesn't make him a gentleman then what does it make him?'

'A blasted idiot,' said Ted. 'Now, Maida, tell me . . . '

'He's just like a boy,' she continued, a soft smile on her lips. 'Just like a great, big, lovable boy. I felt that I just had to kiss him when he said goodnight. It was only a peck on the cheek but he looked so pleased and surprised. I feel so sorry for him in a way. He really needs someone to take care of him.'

'Yes,' said Ted shortly. 'I suppose that he does.' He, like the others, was getting a little tired of hearing how wonderful she thought Robbie was. Norman cleared his throat.

'Did you . . . ' he began when Ted rudely interrupted.

'Allow me,' he snapped, then his voice softened as he turned to Maida. 'Now, dear,' he murmured, 'do you remember what it was you went after?'

'Of course I do.'

'Good. Well, did you get it?'

For a moment they held their breath, releasing it with an audible sigh as Maida rummaged in her handbag and produced the desired object. She held it up on one finger, the heavy metal band glittering as it caught the light, and they stared at it as if it were the Holy Grail.

'He let me look at it,' she smiled. 'He trusted me.'

'And you switched. Good.' Ted reached for the luck machine, his thin, prehensile fingers hooked and ready to grasp the precious thing. Nigel was before him. Like a hungry vulture swooping on a tasty scrap of ten-day dead meat he clawed the object from Maida's hand as Ted was reaching for it. Quickly he slid it over his right hand, adjusting it to his right wrist. Smugly he looked at Ted's outraged expression.

'Got it!'

'You — !' Ted controlled himself with a visible effort but every line of his body yelled the word 'traitor!' Maida swayed a little on her chair and gave a yawn.

'My but I'm tired. I really must go to bed now.'

'I'll come with you,' suggested Nigel. He stepped forward then staggered back as Ted thrust him aside.

'You,' snarled the tall man, 'will stay here. I will see Maida to her room.'

Nigel shrugged and returned to the table. He could afford to be indifferent now that the universe was working on his behalf. Gleefully he touched the machine hugging his wrist and wondered just how long it would take for the thing to reach full potential. Not too long, he imagined. It had begun to work almost at once when Robbie had worn it so he should be able to expect results immediately. Idly he picked up the scattered cards and dealt himself a hand. A flush. Another. Four aces. A third. A full house.

The world, it seemed, was his.

Ted had other ideas. He came barging into the common room a black scowl on his face and murder glinting from his eyes. Rearing over the table he glared down at his friend and fellow conspirator and held out his hand.

'Give.'

'I beg your pardon?' Casually Nigel dealt himself more cards. A straight. He grinned and riffled the deck. 'How about a nice, friendly game of poker?' he suggested. 'I'll accept your I.O.U's.'

'Never mind your damn cards. Give!'

'Give you what, old man?'

'The luck machine! You know very well what I'm getting at. Come on now, pass it over!'

'Why?'

'What?'

'You heard me. Why should I give it to you?'

'So that's the game, is it!' Ted breathed deeply, his hands clenching and his eyes suddenly narrowed. 'For one thing, I made it and, if it belongs to anyone, it belongs to me. For another I don't trust you. Norman and I have a stake in this and we don't intend to stand by and see ourselves robbed. Do you want any more reasons?'

'You don't trust me?' Nigel was astounded. 'Why can't you trust me?' He appealed to Norman. 'You trust me, don't you?'

'Well . . . ' Norman was dubious. 'You did snatch the thing,' he pointed out. 'You didn't give anyone else a chance. Maybe we should draw up an agreement or something before we decide who is to wear it.'

'A contract,' said Ted. 'That's the idea, Norman. We'll draw up a contract and I promise to abide by it to the letter. I won't act like some people I know, mean and selfish and ignorant of the very meaning of the word 'friend'. I won't be greedy once I've got the machine. I am a man of principle and such a man can always be trusted to the hilt.'

'Trusted to do what?' sneered Nigel. 'To look after himself?'

'Never mind all that,' yapped Ted. 'Pass it over and be quick about it!'

'No.' Nigel was stubborn. Nothing could possibly happen to him while he wore the machine and, now that he had the advantage, he intended to keep it. He rose as Ted lunged forward and stepped hastily aside as the table rocked and almost fell. Ted, recovering his balance, looked around and snatched up a poker from the fireplace. He advanced, murder in his eyes.

'Give it to me,' he snarled. 'Now, before I beat your brains out.'

'Norman!' Nigel ducked behind his colleague. 'Don't let him hurt himself!'

'Steady!' Norman grabbed the poker and, without apparent effort, twisted it from Ted's hand and threw it back where it belonged. Stolidly he planted himself before the irate man. 'Don't be a fool, Ted. This is no way to act. One of us has to wear the machine and it might as well be Nigel as you or I.'

'That's right,' said Nigel. 'I don't mind taking the risk. If anything is going to happen then let it happen to me. I'm willing to sacrifice myself for the common good.'

Ted spat a rude word.

'Anyway,' continued Nigel seriously, 'I need it more than either of you. My future happiness depends on it. Maida,' he explained, 'we aren't on the best of terms at the moment. Maybe it's my fault but whether it is or it isn't I need all the luck possible if I hope to get back in favour. So you see, Ted, Norman, it's a question of priority. My need is greater than yours.'

It was too. Maida had acted very strangely and Nigel was worried. Not of Robbie as competition, how could he ever be competition, but because more and more Maida had let him know that he was just so much unwanted furniture cluttering up her life. Now, however, everything would change. Now he owned the luck machine.

He touched it as he left the common room, leaving Ted disconsolate and Norman trying to cheer him up with a column of figures which, in an incredible space of time, would enable them to launch a private rocket ship to the moon — if they wanted to spend their surplus wealth that way. Norman had imagination, he wasn't concerned with the piffling few millions they could win at the racecourses, he was after the big stakes, the stocks and shares which would lead to a financial empire so huge that they would end by, literally, owning the world.

It was a delightful concept but Nigel had even more to look forward to. Gently he touched the band around his wrist as he came in sight of Maida's bedroom door.

Confidently he gripped the handle, twisted and stepped forward. The door stayed where it was.

'Damn!' He stepped back, rubbing his nose, glaring at the blank wooden surface. This was all wrong. The door should have been unlocked at least. His luck should have seen to it that, even if Maida had intended to lock the door, the key should have slipped or she should have forgotten or something happen to prevent his exclusion from the room.

Once again he gripped the knob and once again the door stayed firmly in position. Resisting the desire to shout and beat on the panel, he leaned against the wall and studied the situation.

The luck machine was working for him; fact number one. Therefore there was some reason why the door was not open and, because things were as they were, it was to his advantage that it remain closed; fact number two. Conclusion? He would do more harm than good by seeing Maida at the moment. Luck had prevented him from dropping a first-class brick because, obviously, Maida didn't want to see him now and would only resent him all the more if he tried to force his way inside her room.

The Luck Machine was thwarting his basic desires for his own good.

'Neat,' he murmured as he rubbed the fingers of his left hand over the wide band of the machine. 'Very neat. The thing won't let others hurt you and will stop you from hurting yourself.' He yawned. 'Well, I guess it's too late anyway for that kind of exertion. Still, there's always tomorrow.'

Smothering another huge yawn he ambled his lonely way to bed.

16

The food was ghastly. Ted lifted an egg on the tip of his fork, waved it thoughtfully in the air and then let it fall with a soggy smack to his greasy plate.

'I thought,' he mused, 'that we had managed to convert our fair cook into treating edible comestibles with a little of the respect they deserve.'

'We've been spoiled,' said Norman. He and Ted were the only ones who had appeared in time for breakfast. 'The food has been pretty good these last few days.'

'Then why the sudden change?'

'I don't know.' Norman reached out and piled a slice of bread and butter and marmalade. 'Call it the swing of the pendulum,' he suggested. 'A time of bad food, a time of good food, a time of bad food again. A repetitive cycle which is probably caused by a chain of events beyond human understanding. Have some bread and marmalade.'

'No thanks.' Ted dug at the offending egg with the prongs of his fork. 'Solid,' he announced. 'The yoke broken into the white, the whole thing rendered to the consistency of compressed sponge by the action of heat and then the poor, shattered, insulted fruit of the hen basted in what seemed to be engine oil. Something will have to be done about Alice.'

'Why worry?' Norman helped himself to more bread and marmalade. 'In a few days we'll be breakfasting on caviare and champagne.' He looked thoughtful. 'You know,' he said, 'I'm not so sure that I would like that. Pretty sickening stuff for first thing in the morning.'

'You'll get used to it,' assured Ted as if he had eaten it all his life. He leaned back, his eyes dreamy behind their spectacles. 'A French chef,' he decided, 'or maybe two of them. Or, better still, we'll buy the swankiest hotel in London, kick out the guests, keep on the staff and use it as our town dwelling. One of our town dwellings,' he amended. 'We could let some of our friends stay there when we weren't using it.'

'Maida would like that.' Norman glanced at his wrist-watch and frowned. 'Odd that she isn't down yet. It isn't like her to be so late.'

'The poor girl was up very late last night,' said Ted magnanimously. 'We all were. Personally I had trouble getting to sleep for wondering about an important matter. Would you,' he asked seriously, 'go in for a Rolls or a Cadillac? Both have their good points and I can't decide which to choose. Of course, there is nothing quite like a Rolls from the prestige point of view but, well, they are rather staid. A Cadillac seems to attract the girls, the New World status symbol, you know. So . . . '

'Have one of each,' advised Norman with his usual good sense. He frowned at his watch again. 'No sign of Nigel either. Do you think — ?'

'No!' Ted sprang to his feet, an anguished expression on his face. 'No! He wouldn't! He couldn't! The dirty swine! If he's run out on us I'll — !' Gasping, unable to finish the sentence for the emotion which choked him, he stood, pawing at the air and then, with a peculiar croak, lunged towards the door.

Norman, determined to protect his investment, followed at his heels.

'You take the stairs,' snapped Ted. 'I'll check the back. The first one to find him brings him down to the common room. Hurry!'

'Wait!' Norman, one foot on the stairs leading to the upstairs bedrooms, stared upwards with a startled expression on his face. 'Here he is.'

A figure lurched down the stairs. It clung to the handrail and moved as if something had crushed, trampled and kicked it into an overall state of decrepitude. It stared at them from lack-lustre eyes from a face that was ghastly in its pallor. It looked, Norman thought, like a tailor's dummy which had been exposed to heat so that all the stiffening had run out leaving only the padding. A tailor's dummy, that is, that had been dressed like a respectable scarecrow.

'Nigel!' Ted, ever solicitous for the

welfare of his friend, sprang forward and grabbed him as he reached the foot of the stairs. A brief examination calmed his fears, the metal band still hugged the limp right wrist. 'Nigel, old chap, what's the matter?'

'He's ill,' said Norman. 'Shall I call the doctor?'

'He's in shock,' decided Ted as Nigel opened his mouth and gasped like a fish. 'Get him inside and pour some of that coffee down his throat.'

The coffee was vile. Anyone drinking it would either be devoid of taste buds, vomit or recover sufficiently to act in his own defence. Weakly Nigel pushed away the second cup Ted held to his mouth.

'She's gone!' he croaked.

'Gone?'

'Maida. She's gone.'

'Oh!' Ted looked thoughtful for a moment then, as he glanced at Nigel's wrist, managed to recover his aplomb. 'Ah, well, never mind,' he said brightly. 'We still have the luck machine.'

Norman was more sympathetic.

'How do you mean, gone?' he demanded.

'Maybe she stepped out for a walk or something.'

'She's left me,' groaned Nigel. 'She's run off with Robbie.'

'With whom?'

'Robbie.'

'I don't believe it,' yapped Ted. 'I simply don't believe it.'

'Why not?' asked Nigel viciously. 'Because you hoped that she would run off with you?' The coffee had worked wonders. He still looked far from his normal self but, at least, he looked more human than he had before the crude first-aid. 'Is that what's upsetting you, Ted?'

'Well . . . ' Ted looked abashed for a moment then quickly recovered. 'Well now, Nigel, that's absolute nonsense and you must know it. How could you ever think that I'd do a thing like that to one of my best friends. Why, the idea is ridiculous.'

'Not so ridiculous. But it doesn't matter now. She's gone. They've both gone.'

'Did she give any reason?' asked

Norman. 'Did you see her or did she leave a note?'

'A note.'

'May we read it?' Norman took the folded sheet of paper and, jerking his head at Ted, crossed to the far side of the room. Together they read the hasty scrawl.

'My dear Nigel,' the letter commenced. 'This will probably come as a shock to you but it should not come as a surprise. For a long time now our marriage hasn't been all that it should have been and, as I warned you, it could not have lasted much longer unless you did something to alter the situation. Well, that is no longer necessary. I have found the man I have been looking for all my life. Eric is a wonderful person and I cannot understand how I have known him for so long without recognizing his sterling qualities. He needs me, more now than ever, to save him from false friends and those who would exploit his good luck. We are going to Mexico where I shall divorce you and marry Eric. We shall never part. Sincerely yours, Maida.'

'The soldier's farewell,' said Ted sourly. 'Poor old Nigel. I never thought that Maida could be such a bitch.'

'Maybe she couldn't help herself?' Norman's voice held a peculiar inflexion. Ted frowned as he slowly folded the note.

'Last night,' he mused. 'She acted odd. I thought that she was a little intoxicated.'

'She wasn't drunk.' Norman kept his voice low in consideration of his colleague. 'She was in love.'

'With Robbie? But why? How?'

'Let's be logical about this. You said yourself that his weakness was women. Naturally he was attracted to her, how could he help himself?'

'All right, but that was him to her. What the hell made her fall for him?' Ted froze, staring at Norman with a horrified expression. Norman, too much a gentleman to interrupt, waited for the penny to drop. 'The luck machine!' Ted tore at his hair. 'That blasted luck machine!'

'Of course.' A cloud of smoke rose as Norman lit his pipe. 'What is the most unlucky thing that could ever happen to a man? Isn't it to fall in love with a woman who wants no part of him? Unrequited love, the most painful emotion there is. How could Robbie's luck have been so bad?'

'It couldn't. Not with the machine working for him. Maida simply had to fall in love with him, she couldn't help herself, not once he had fallen in love with her.'

'Exactly.'

'But, wait a minute,' Ted was excited. 'Maida switched the machine. Nigel is wearing it now and he should be the one getting the luck. He . . . ' Ted broke off, a dreadful expression on his face. 'Nigel!'

'Uh?'

'Nigel, you damned idiot! Give me the machine.'

'No!' Nigel yelped as Ted advanced on him. 'You stay away from me! Norman! Help!'

'Yes, Norman, help.' Ted breathed hard as his hands clamped on his wriggling victim. 'Help me get the thing off him so that we can see what happened. Stop struggling, Nigel. Damn it, I only want to look!'

He had worked for days on the substitute. He had deliberately wasted time so as to give Maida an opportunity to use her charms on Robbie but, even so, he had fashioned an exact facsimile. Exact, that is, but for one tiny intended flaw. The air turned blue as he found it.

'Hoodwinked,' he yelled. 'We've been hoodwinked!'

'Not deliberately.' Norman, as ever, remained phenomenally calm. 'Robbie passed Maida the luck machine, she, probably, fully intended to switch them but Robbie's luck was still strong. She mixed them up. She gave him back the original luck machine and gave us the substitute. We never,' he added delicately, 'had the opportunity to check on the success of the operation.'

'No,' snarled Ted. 'We didn't, did we? And why? Because our trusted and respected colleague here turned out to be the worst kind of grasping opportunist I've ever had the misfortune to meet. Would he allow me to examine the machine? Oh, no! He wouldn't trust his old friend. Friend!' Ted almost spat the word. 'A fine way to treat a friend! I wouldn't be so harsh to a dog.'

'And what about you!' yelled Nigel, stung from his apathy. 'Who's brilliant idea was it in the first place? Who was too blind and conceited to think of what must happen once those two got together? Friend!' It was his turn to spit. 'Some friend. He's cost me my wife, that's all!'

'Now, now,' soothed Norman. 'There's no sense in tearing into each other. No one is really to blame. Once Robbie got that machine on his wrist there was nothing we could do. He was lucky, that's all, but that covers everything. He was lucky because the machine worked and is working. In fact he is really the luckiest man alive today.'

'God!' Ted slumped down at the table and rested his head in his hands. 'Have you thought of what's going to happen now?'

'They will go to Mexico,' said Norman. 'He has our winnings to get them there and leave some over for investment.'

'Maida is ambitious,' mused Nigel. 'That was one of our troubles. She has always been interested in politics.'

'Mexico and the South American States are hotbeds of revolution,' added Norman. 'A lucky man, a man like Robbie, could easily be elected to power and wind up as a minor dictator.'

'He wouldn't stay minor for long,' qualified Ted gloomily. 'The luck machine is progressive, don't forget. He will go on and on getting luckier and luckier all the time. He could end up by conquering the world.'

'That's very true, logically it's inescapable.' Norman stared interestedly at the stem of his pipe. 'You know,' he said casually, 'it is an observed fact that a person in power will always try to inflict his own ideas of right and wrong, ethics and morality on his subjects. Robbie, in his way, is rather a fanatic.'

'He doesn't smoke,' pointed out Nigel.

'Nor gamble.'

'Nor touch alcohol.'

'And he has firm ideas on the dress and conduct of women. No!' Nigel shook his head as he thought about it. 'The South Americans are a logical people. They'll never let him get so far. They'll shoot him or bomb him or stab him or something.'

'The luckiest man in the world?' Ted was more of a realist than Nigel and far less an optimist. 'How? They won't be able to touch him. In fact,' he added with awe, 'Robbie could well go on forever. He could be immortal!'

'Yes,' said Norman.

'That's right,' said Nigel.

Together the three of them sat and pondered on the end of their world.

THE END

We do hope that you have enjoyed reading this large print book.

Did you know that all of our titles are available for purchase?

We publish a wide range of high quality large print books including:
Romances, Mysteries, Classics
General Fiction
Non Fiction and Westerns

Special interest titles available in large print are:
The Little Oxford Dictionary
Music Book, Song Book
Hymn Book, Service Book

Also available from us courtesy of Oxford University Press:
Young Readers' Dictionary
(large print edition)
Young Readers' Thesaurus
(large print edition)

For further information or a free brochure, please contact us at:
Ulverscroft Large Print Books Ltd.,
The Green, Bradgate Road, Anstey,
Leicester, LE7 7FU, England.
Tel: (00 44) **0116 236 4325**
Fax: (00 44) **0116 234 0205**

Other titles in the
Linford Mystery Library:

MAN OF TWO WORLDS

John Russell Fearn

Walter Cardish was a very ordinary, somewhat downtrodden individual. But, following an incredible accident, he recovers in hospital and finds that he has been granted the power of seeing into the future. Assuming the identity of 'The Great Volta: Prognosticator' he amasses a fortune, and a reputation as a seer. But his activities also create enemies, and soon one of them tries to kill him, and the implacable workings of his strange destiny close in upon him inexorably . . .

SHERLOCK HOLMES AND THE CROSBY MURDERS

Gary Lovisi

The glamorous actress Susan Copely is being persecuted — and the reason lies in the events surrounding the wreck of the *Sophy Anderson* two decades before . . . A well-regarded businessman appears to have brutally stabbed his wife to death, and then suffocated their two small children before fleeing their home. But Holmes, deploying his unique investigative methods, is set upon proving otherwise . . . Finally, a most singular narrative from Mycroft Holmes at last sheds light upon what truly happened at the Reichenbach Falls that fateful day in 1891 . . .

THE CHRONICLES OF SHERLOCK HOLMES

Paul D. Gilbert

Dr John Watson reveals unchronicled cases only previously alluded to: The Baron Maupertuis, The Remarkable Disappearance of James Phillimore, The Aluminium Crutch, The Abominable Wife, The Cutter *Alicia*, The Red Leech and The Mumbling Duellist . . . What is the connection between an impoverished dowager, an attempt on Mycroft's life and Holmes's deadliest adversary? Can Holmes discover if a ship really disappeared in a patch of mist or is his client's father insane? And who or what is the red leech?